A Match Made in Montana

A Match Made in Montana

A Millers of Marietta Romance

Elsa Winckler

TULE
PUBLISHING

Chapter One

"*DAMN YOU'RE KILLING me,*" *he groaned. His gaze dropped to where her beautiful breasts strained against the top, the hard beads of her nipples tantalizingly visible...*

Laughing softly and fanning herself, Annie looked down at her own breasts. "No visible beads, tantalizing or otherwise," she said out loud touching her one breast.

Still grinning, she picked up the book again. This was why she loved reading romance novels. It was pure fantasy. Dashing heroes, strong heroines, beautiful settings—what was not to like? And of course, she enjoyed the steamy sex scenes, especially since her arrival in Marietta.

Moving across state lines from Sacramento to Montana, and then living for months amidst the chaos of the renovation of her B and B, didn't leave time for much else, let alone steamy encounters with dashing heroes. The only steamy scenes she encountered nowadays were in the kitchen.

Besides, her one experience with love had left her a little bruised and skeptical about the existence of soul mates and the kind of love portrayed in stories. In a romance novel, no hero worth his salt would text his heroine weeks before the wedding saying he'd met someone else, telling her men no longer want to marry women who only wanted to stay at home and cook.

That did, apparently, happen in real life though. Had happened to her. Dropping the book on her chest she looked up at Copper Mountain rising high above the small town of Marietta she now had the privilege to call home.

If she were honest, not getting to marry Ted Harris was probably one of the best things that could've happened to her.

It took her a while but after the initial shock and hurt of Ted's rejection had subsided, she'd realized she'd loved the idea of getting married much more that she'd ever loved Ted. He certainly hadn't been the second half that would made her whole as Plato had explained the idea of soul mates centuries ago.

Not everybody was as lucky as her sister Vivian who'd found someone like Aiden who understood her and loved her, warts and all. Annie sighed. Maybe not everybody was destined to find a soul mate.

Looking down at her breasts again, a giggle slipped out. Ted's quick and uninspiring pecks certainly never had the power to get her nipples to bead.

Laughing softly again, she checked her watch. She had a dinner to start, not lay around reading about kissing and unattainable sexy heroes and letting loose the busy beetles that seemed to occupy her mind.

Janice had also said she'd be stopping by for a quick cup. Janice O'Sullivan, music teacher and also godmother to Annie's soon to be brother-in-law Aiden, was one of the first people who'd welcomed Annie and her siblings, Mitch and Vivian, in Marietta. Janice was also helping with the arrangements for Vivian and Aiden's wedding; she probably wanted to talk about that.

Inhaling deeply, Annie closed her eyes. Surely, a few more lazy minutes wouldn't make such a difference.

It was the end of April, the bitter cold of February had, thank goodness, been replaced with milder temperatures. Moving here from warm temperatures of California, the harsher weather conditions in winter came as quite a shock to all of them.

Fortunately, spring was on its way and, while it was still cold at night, the days were milder. This part of the porch, she'd discovered, got direct sunlight throughout the day, the ideal place to put up a hammock for her guests. Unfortunately, the many guests she'd envisaged visiting her B and B and writing swooning reviews about her food, had yet to arrive.

She'd really hoped by now, two months after the renovation of the house had been completed, her phone would be ringing off the hook and her email box would be brimming with requests from potential guests, but apart from a few visitors over the Valentine's weekend, it had been quiet. She'd have to find other ways to advertise than just using her website and one online marketplace—that was becoming crystal clear. The truth was, if she wanted to stay in business, she'd need more visitors.

The Spring Arts and Crafts Festival was in ten days' time and she hadn't had a single booking so far.

The reason she'd studied to be a chef was mainly so, somewhere along the way, she'd run her own B and B and she could cook for people. She loved doing that, especially for those close to her.

Now her dream had come true, but how to get guests to come and stay here—that was the big question. For the moment, she was still doing okay. Vivian and Aiden were staying here and paying rent while the house they'd bought close by was being renovated. It should be finished by the time they got married in two weeks' time. Mitch, her brother, was also still living with her and paying rent, but he'd probably also find a place of his own soon.

When Aiden and Vivian moved out, she'd have a problem if she didn't get more paying guests soon. She'd used her part of their inheritance from their parents to renovate the house. At the moment she still had money in the bank, but it wouldn't last forever.

There had to be a solution to her problem. Maybe she could ask Craig, Aiden's cousin, to help her? As soon as the thought popped up though, she repressed it. Ludicrous idea. He was in marketing and a big shot at some or other well-known firm in Portland. Janice liked to brag. Helping a struggling B and B owner would so not be something he'd be interested in doing. Besides, she'd seen him only once when he and Riley, his cousin and Aiden's sister had been visiting.

Truth be told, the big redheaded Irishman had left her a bit unsettled. Hugging her goodbye when they'd just met— she still wasn't sure how she felt about those few milliseconds up close and personal with him.

Rolling her eyes, she spoke out loud again. "Focus, Annie, focus. Thinking about sexy Irishmen is not going to help."

Marketing, that was what she should be concentrating on. On Vivian's suggestion, she'd listed Annie's on a well-known marketing place, hoping to attract visitors who would write reviews. However, up until now, there hadn't been any queries, let alone reviews.

Social media? She groaned out loud. As a last resort. Maybe. She'd never seen the point of sharing every aspect of her life with strangers, seriously. Selling Annie's though, was also not an option, not after all the renovations and time she'd spent turning it into a friendly, welcoming place. Maybe she should give social media a try. Or another marketing website. Looking around her, she sighed. She loved this place, she had to try and hold on to it.

After their parents' untimely demise her brother, Mitch had the idea they should relocate to another state. She'd remembered this beautiful town they'd visited with their parents when they were all still at school and when she'd found this house for sale, she knew this was where she wanted to have the B and B she'd always dreamed of.

This place was her happy ending, a place where she could remember Mom and Dad. For a moment, she was reminded of the horrible way they'd died, but she inhaled deeply, willing the sad thoughts away.

She and Mitch and Vivian had all seen a psychologist in Bozeman over the last few months and, although getting over the pain of losing their parents was not a quick fix, she was grateful all three of them were on the journey. She'd also found peace in her daily routine, in the beautiful town they now called home and in the many friends she'd made since moving here.

Happy endings, she'd come to realize after her encounter with that elusive thing called love, didn't always mean a husband and kids. It could also mean having a B and B filled with guests enjoying her food.

The problem was getting the house filled. She had book-ings, but at this point it still was only when Bramble House Bed-and-Breakfast, the famous three-story Victorian house down the road from Annie's, was fully booked.

"*Aargh.*" She groaned out loud, rubbing her nose. "May-be it hadn't been a good idea to have another B and B in a town the size of Marietta. Maybe—"

"Hi, Annie." Someone chuckled close by. "You always talk to yourself?"

Annie's eyes flew open and, as she struggled to sit upright, the hammock swayed, she lost her balance, the book fell to the ground. Arms flaying, she tried to regain some control over her limbs so she wouldn't actually fall. Seriously, not in front of Craig O'Sullivan, the very man she'd been thinking about.

Big, strong hands caught her just as she was about to tumble to the ground. Before she could catch her breath, she was pulled tightly against a solid wall of muscles rippling against her cheek. Wow. He'd hugged her once before, but it was a quick one, over before it had quite begun. He had to work out, nobody could be this toned and not work out. Maybe she should check…

Sanity fortunately prevailed a millisecond before she actually put a hand out to test whether what she'd felt against her face were really muscles. Appalled at herself, she quickly stepped back. She'd been standing close to him for much longer than need be, what was she thinking? Hard body, rippling muscles—that was what she'd been thinking. A favorite description in those romances she loved to read. Oh, dear, so not something she should be thinking about right now. She didn't even know the man.

Out of the corner of her eye, she caught a glimpse of the book she'd been reading, lying where it had fallen on the ground. Hopefully he hadn't seen that.

"Craig…" She was out of breath. Seriously. Trying to pull herself together, she did her best to sound be like a successful B and B owner. "I wasn't expecting you. How long … have you been here a while?"

His eyes were still twinkling. "Yes."

She felt like rolling her eyes but stopped herself in time. The one-syllable guy, she'd forgotten. "So you've heard …" She motioned with her hand toward the hammock.

"About beads and sexy Irishmen? Indeed."

Her face flamed, but she tried to ignore it. "You should've told me earlier you were here. How can I help you? You haven't made a reservation that I know of."

"I'm staying with Aunt Janice."

"Wow, an actual sentence with a verb and everything," she got out, sounding more sarcastic than she'd intended. If she'd been in her kitchen making dinner, she wouldn't have been literally falling at the Irishman's feet and she wouldn't be at such a disadvantage and consequently be so mad at herself. "Sorry, didn't mean to snap. Okay, if you don't want a room…"

But he wasn't looking at her; he was bending down to pick up the book she'd been reading. It was one of those earth-please-open-up-and-let-me-disappear moments. She wasn't embarrassed to be caught reading a romance novel. It was just that this particular one had the picture of a very sexy guy on the cover. Naked torso, rippling muscles, sexy grin— the works. Also not something she was embarrassed about— usually. But having been plastered against a very similar torso minutes ago was making this situation awkward, to say the least.

"Interesting reading," he said, turning the book over. He'd picked it up as it had been lying on the floor—open. His eyes skimmed over the page before he closed the book and handed it back to her.

Face flaming again, she just about grabbed the book out of his hands. He'd read the page, she was sure of it. And was it her imagination or was he checking out her breasts? In the next millisecond, she froze, her breath hitching way back in her throat. What was happening? Surely, her nipples weren't actually *beading*?

Quickly turning away, she glanced down at herself. *Oh, my. Look at that.* They were doing something very close to beading! This was ridiculous, seriously. She stopped herself just in time from touching her breasts again. Without looking back, she rushed toward her kitchen, her safe place. Hopefully the freaking beading would stop.

"Coffee? Tea?" she called out over her shoulder.

Another chuckle from behind her, but no words. She didn't dare turn back to face him. As she entered the kitchen, she put down the book on the counter, grabbed the sweater hanging over a chair and pulled it on over her head, sending a silent prayer it would cover her tell-tale breasts.

Still no sound from behind her. Filling the kettle, she began to talk. "You're a bit early for the wedding, aren't you? Is Riley with you? How is Janice? I haven't seen her in a while, we've been so busy. I've been expecting her, do you know..."

She turned around to find Craig's deep blue eyes resting on her.

CRAIG HAD A hard time—and not only figuratively speaking—not grabbing Annie and kissing her. Watching her touching her breasts... The innocent movement nearly had him falling at her feet. Man, he definitely needed to get out more.

He'd met Annie in February when he and his cousin Riley had stayed in Annie's B and B for one night. Their main reason for the trip had been to make sure Aiden didn't let Vivian slip through his fingers.

Because Aunt Janice had been busy helping with the Valentine's ball, Riley had booked rooms for them at Annie's after she'd discovered Aiden's love interest had a sister with a B and B.

During the day and a half he and Riley had stayed here, he'd never seen Annie this flustered. She was the calm one, the nurturing one, making sure everyone around her was happy. Or wait... On impulse, he'd hugged her just before they'd left. She'd blushed and had been clearly rattled by the hug.

So, what had disturbed her usual equilibrium this time? The steamy book she'd been reading, her near fall to the floor? And who was the sexy Irishman she'd been mumbling about? He didn't know, but he was … intrigued.

What he did know for sure was that for a moment there, standing in front of him, she'd been aroused which in turn had aroused him. Again. Hence the ridiculous thought to kiss her.

His reaction probably had a lot to do with the fact that Annie had, strangely enough, occupied a big part of his thoughts over the last two months since he'd seen her. Usually, he was focused either on his job or on whether Riley or Aiden were okay, but at odd times he'd found himself thinking about the brunette with the big brown eyes and the most beautiful smile he'd ever seen.

Could it be she was also the main reason he'd agreed to visit Aunt Janice two weeks before Aiden and Vivian's wedding? Or was the restlessness he'd been experiencing over the last few months the reason?

He'd always loved his job in advertising and marketing. He loved the creative aspect of it, the brainstorming, the developing of the plan, taking it to the client and seeing their faces when they saw ideas transformed into practice. It was the other side of the business, having to constantly compete, to be always one step ahead of the rest, that was getting to him. Especially after this last account they'd managed to grab from another competitor. This time he'd been made aware of the consequences for the other company. It had left him uneasy and troubled.

Under usual circumstances, he wouldn't have dreamt of

taking leave and flying to Bozeman to spend two weeks with his aunt. He hadn't realized how much he needed to get away until he'd received his aunt's message.

She'd sent a long message to him and Riley telling them there was so much to be done before the big day, it would be nice to have both or at least one of them around to help. And if Aunt Janice asked they helped. She'd been there for them when they'd needed her. Riley was preparing for an exhibition that opened at the end of May, after Aiden's wedding, so much to his cousin's amazement, he'd agreed to take leave from work and go and help their aunt.

He never took time away from work, but lately his office seemed to have shrunk, became claustrophobic, making it hard to breathe. The chance to get away for a few weeks, see his aunt, help his cousin get married, and maybe see the lovely Annie Miller as well, had seemed like good reasons to take a much-needed break.

Apart from maybe Riley, there wasn't anyone in Portland who'd miss him. He had a strictly two-date rule and usually dated more than one woman at a time. He wasn't interested in getting married, having kids, and settling down in the suburbs with a white picket fence—something he spelled out whenever he dated someone.

"Um ... do you know if Janice is also on her way?" Annie asked.

He frowned. A strange question. "Janice said you wanted to talk to me."

Clearly confused, she stared at him. "No, she—"

Just then her phone rang. "It's Janice," she said. "Just a moment. Hi, Janice, I was—" Annie darted a look toward him. "Yes, he's just arrived, but…"

Silence. Her mouth opened a few times to say something, but Aunt Janice seemed to be on a roll.

Finally, she managed a few words. "But, Janice, I can't impose—"

Cut short again, Annie walked toward the kitchen window while talking, giving him a chance to study her. Tall and slender, her long hair in a messy ponytail. As he watched, she pulled out the elastic holding it in place. Her hair tumbled down way past her shoulders, the brown hues altering as the strands curled and moved with the nodding of her head. Inside of him, something moved.

"Janice, I really appreciate your suggestion, but…" Another glance in his direction before she reluctantly nodded. "Okay, I'll do that. Thank you."

Chewing on her lower lip, she approached him.

That was something else he hadn't been able to stop thinking about—the way she would chew on her full lower lip whenever she was worried or anxious about anything.

"I'm so sorry about this. Janice means well, I know, but … now you've wasted your time."

"So, you don't want to talk to me?"

"It's not that I don't want—" She rubbed her face. "Janice, bless her heart, wants to help me. I've been moaning about the lack of visitors to my B and B, Janice has probably heard about it and thought you could help me with market-ing, which of course, is a ludicrous idea. Now you've wasted your time and all for nothing."

"Why ludicrous?"

She threw up her hand. "Because you're … you. A sexy, hotshot marketing guru from a big firm in Portland and I'm a nobody with a B and B in Marietta, a town most people probably haven't heard of before."

His brows shot up. "Sexy?"

Her face was flaming and she turned away, covering her cheeks with her hands. "I can't believe that's all you got from what I've just said. It's not that I think you're sexy … I mean, of course, you are but…"

Moving forward quickly, he tried to stop the chuckle from escaping, but he was going to lose the battle.

Chapter Two

ANNIE ROUNDED ON Craig. "It's not funny!" She'd thought he was still standing on the other side of her kitchen, but he'd moved so that he was right behind her, their faces now inches apart.

Lifting a hand, he tucked a curl behind her ear, long fingers skimming her face as he dropped his arm. "I've never been called sexy before. And you, Annie Miller, may be many things, but a nobody isn't one of them. You're one of a kind."

Had he moved closer still or was that her imagination? She had to say something, anything, but her mouth was so dry, she wouldn't get a word out if she tried. Slipping out her tongue, she licked her lips.

His breath hitched, his eyes dropped to her mouth and, oh, my goodness, if she wasn't mistaken, there was more beading happening. Fortunately, she'd put on another layer of clothes, hopefully he wouldn't notice it.

Just then, his eyes dropped further, and she lost her breath. He looked up, his blue eyes darkened with an expression she'd never seen before.

"Craig?" a voice said from somewhere far away. "I didn't know you were here. When did you arrive in Marietta?"

With a last smoldering look at her, Craig turned around. "Hi, Aiden."

Smoldering? There was no smoldering. What was she thinking? While the cousins were talking, she quickly looked down at her boobs. *Oh, my goodness, what's up with the beading?* To make it worse, the extra top wasn't helping to cover it up. Why was she still stuck on the freaking word? Surely there were other ways to describe what was happening. Nipples hardened and… For the life of her, she couldn't think of another expression.

Flustered, she turned around and reached for the kettle. Turning on the tap, she began to fill it with water. Why was she still thinking about her boobs? Maybe because they felt strangely heavy?

"Um, Annie?"

She looked up to see Vivian looking strangely at her. "What?"

Grinning, Vivian looked down. "I don't think the kettle needs more water."

Annie looked down to see the kettle filled to the brim.

"Why don't you sit down, I'll make tea?" Vivian said, clearly amused.

Annie ignored her sister's grin. "I'll make the tea. You can get the cups. Who wants tea?"

Aiden pulled out a chair. "Thanks, Annie. That sounds

great. Craig?"

"Yes, please."

Annie didn't turn around but heard another chair being pulled out. She was being absurd. Rinsing the teapot, she took a few deep breaths before she measured out the tea to put in the pot. The normal, everyday task managed to calm her down. Somewhat.

"I'm very happy to see you," Aiden was saying to Craig, "but I can't believe you've actually left your office."

"Aunt Janice asked. Said she needed help with the wedding."

"Really?" Aiden asked and looked at his fiancé. "Vivian? Do you know with what she still needs help? The hotel does most of it, there really isn't that much to do. She could've asked me, I'm not sure … except…" Laughing, he slapped Craig on the shoulder. "You know what I think?"

"What?" Craig asked.

The tea was made and Annie finally felt comfortable enough to turn around. Vivian had also taken a seat next to Aiden.

"You don't think she's trying out her matchmaking skills again?" Aiden asked. "She's still denying it, but I still think the reason she'd invited me here was so that I could meet Vivian. You remember what she used to say? 'When you're Irish, matchmaking was a skill you were born with.' Not that I'm complaining, mind you, but I'm still pretty sure my meeting Vivian was her idea. Has she mentioned any women she wanted to introduce you to?"

Craig met Annie's eyes. "She said Annie wanted to talk to me but…"

Annie put down the teapot. This was getting more bizarre by the minute. "She is trying to help me. That's all. I'm not a candidate for any matchmaker."

"Help you, how?" Vivian asked.

"With marketing the B and B. She suggested I should get Craig to help me."

Vivian's eyes were twinkling. "Oh, yeah, it definitely sounds as if she's only trying to help you." Before Annie could stop her sister, she turned toward Craig. "So how about it, Craig? Can you help Annie?"

"Don't be silly. Craig can't—"

"I'm happy to help," Craig interrupted. "But Annie thinks I'm too…"

Blue eyes met hers and she inhaled sharply. Surely, he wasn't going to tell everyone she'd called him sexy?

"I can't remember the word she used but she thinks I'm too…" Craig continued.

"Busy," she quickly interjected. "He's from a big firm in Portland. I have a small B and B. It's so not what he does."

"Well, he's here for the next two weeks," Vivian said, her eyes full of mirth. "You should use him."

Annie could cheerfully throttle her sister. Not only was she putting her in a very awkward position, but now several vivid, inappropriate images of exactly how she could "use"

Craig were running through her mind. It was all those freaking romances she'd been reading. She should burn the lot of them.

She picked up the pot. "More tea, anyone?"

Grinning, Aiden lifted his empty cup. "We haven't had the first cup yet, Annie."

Mortified, Annie put the teapot down. "Viv, would you pour? Excuse me for a moment, please?" And with as much dignity as she could muster under the circumstances, she walked out of her kitchen. She definitely needed a minute away from Craig O'Sullivan's smoldering eyes. Smoldering? There was no smoldering. Why did the word keep popping in her head?

IGNORING AIDEN AND Vivian's amused glances, Craig held his cup for Vivian to pour him tea.

"So, can you help her?" Vivian asked as she moved to Aiden.

"Of course. But she doesn't want my help. I'm here for the next two weeks, I can help with the wedding, though."

Vivian put the pot down. "The wedding preparations are on track, thank you. If you can persuade Annie to let you help her with her marketing, it would be great."

"What does she do to advertise?" Craig asked.

"She has a website and she advertises on a marketplace

I've told her about as far as I know."

"Nothing on social media?" She wasn't, he knew that, he'd already checked, but it was a question he should be asking. Annie might be using a different name.

Vivian shook her head. "She's not on social media. Hates it."

As he picked up his cup, Annie walked back into the kitchen. She'd taken off the extra sweater she'd put on, her hair was back in a tidy ponytail and her smile was back in place. "There are still scones left over from this morning … anyone?"

"No thanks," said Vivian. "It's too close to dinner and I have a wedding dress that I need to fit into in two weeks' time."

Patting his tummy, Aiden also stood up. "Not for me either, thanks, Annie. I've gained so much weight since I've lived here. You're a great cook."

"It's a good thing," Vivian teased, taking his arm. "I'm not much of a cook."

"Fortunately, I'm not marrying you for your cooking." Aiden grinned as they left the kitchen. "See you, coz!" he called out over his shoulder.

"Annie, listen to Craig. He's willing to help," Vivian said as they left.

For a few moments it was quiet in the kitchen. Annie was the first to speak.

"What about you? You want a scone?"

At least she was looking at him again. He shook his head. "I'm here for two weeks. Aidan and Vivian don't need help with the wedding. I can help you."

"Thank you for the offer but we both know marketing a B and B in a very small town is so not what you do."

"What if I tell you that it's exactly the kind of thing I won't mind doing right now?"

"I won't believe you. You work with huge corporations and companies and huge budgets…"

"Exactly. This would be a welcoming change." He pressed his lips together before he continued. "I've had enough of the dog-eats-dog scene for the moment. The last account we've secured had left a bitter taste in my mouth."

"What happened?"

"The competition was a small firm. They had to close down. Usually, I won't even know what happens to the firms we've competed with for an account, but this time I became aware of the consequences. Ever since…" Grimacing, he shook his head. "I don't know why I'm telling you this, I haven't spoken to anyone about it."

"Sometimes it's easier to discuss things with strangers. I'm sorry about what happened, but surely you have other projects you're working on?"

"I do. There's a whole team working on it. I'm keeping track of what is happening. I have time to help you." What was he doing? Just about begging Annie to let him help her? He quickly got up. "I can help you make a success of your B and B or you can go back to reading about the tantalizing hard beads in your book. Your choice."

Inhaling sharply, she glared at him. "I can't believe you've read that!"

Grinning, he approached her slowly. "I had to know what made you so hot and bothered."

"I wasn't hot and bothered!" she exclaimed, waving her hands in front of her.

Without really thinking about what he was doing, he took her hands in his and pulled her closer. She stilled, looked up at him, her brown eyes turning from outrage to being wary and something else he couldn't quite put his finger on. A soft flowery scent mixed with something citrusy floated around them.

He'd wanted to touch her. Truth be told, he'd been wanting to touch her since he'd stepped on to the porch. The memory of his fingers trailing over a soft cheek had been begging him to touch her again.

Like earlier, his eyes dropped lower. Her body was reacting to his nearness the same way he was reacting to her. The very obvious sign of his desire throbbing against her was not something he could hide.

Throbbing—where the hell did that word come from? *The damn book she'd been reading, that's where.*

"Will you look at that?" He chuckled. "It would seem our bodies like each other. Is that the beading you've been reading about?"

Inhaling sharply, Annie pulled her hands from his and turned away. "I don't know what you're talking about." She picked up a cloth, dropped it, picked it up again. "So, how do you think you can help me?"

This time he laughed out loud. "That's a loaded question. There are so many ways…"

"I'm talking about the B and B," she said crossly.

"I know." He smiled slowly walking closer to her. "I'm just teasing."

As she turned toward him again, she moved away and held up a hand. "Stay right there, don't come closer. You … you fluster me. And stop talking about beading!"

He really tried, but he couldn't stop the smile.

Avoiding his eyes, she took a deep breath. "You're way out of my league. Besides, you … when you're near me, I … there's the … the beading … damn it, I can't believe I'm stuck on that word! There are these strange feelings and I … well, I don't like it. So, no, I don't think it's a good idea."

Chuckling, Craig took a step back. "Is this better?"

She nodded but avoided his eyes.

"I could have a look at your website and maybe make a few suggestions? We don't even have to be in the same room."

"I appreciate the offer, but I'll be okay. Janice means well and I'll be sure to tell her you've offered to help, don't worry."

Craig opened his mouth to try and convince her to let

him help her, but he stopped just in time. What the hell was he doing? He was here for Aunt Janice. Besides, Annie was right. Working closely with this gorgeous woman was not a good idea.

Those strange feelings she'd been talking about? He also didn't like the way she managed to get him all hot and bothered with just a smile.

CROSS, ANNIE GLARED at the door through which Craig had just walked. Who had given him the right to come in here…

"Talking to yourself again, Annie?" Vivian said, entering from the back door.

Pressing her lips together, Annie gathered the last of the cups. "Just thinking out loud," she muttered.

"You were awfully flustered just now. Has anything happened between you and Craig I should know of?"

"Of course not!" Annie called out too quickly.

Vivian chuckled. "I can quote Shakespeare…"

"It's all Janice's fault. I know she's just being nice, but sending Craig to come and help me with marketing is a ridiculous idea. He works with huge companies and budgets. Apart from anything else, I don't have any money to pay him."

"You don't have anything to lose by asking him for suggestions. I'm sure he wouldn't think of charging you for that."

"Well, I'm not going to, so can we drop it, please? Tell me about your house? Do you think it'll be ready by the time you get married?"

Shaking her head, Vivian laughed. "Oh, no, we're not changing the subject this quickly. The kitchen was alive with strange vibes just now."

"The only vibes you're feeling are the ones between you and Aiden."

Vivian shook her head. "Nope, sorry, but this was different. I've never seen you this rattled. What happened? Come, on, sis, it's me. Your sister."

Groaning, Annie threw up her hands. "Nothing happened. I was reading on the porch when he arrived. I nearly fell from the hammock, he helped me. That's it."

"So why are you blushing when you mention falling from the hammock?"

"I was reading a romance novel and it was … awkward."

Peals of Vivian's laughter filled the kitchen.

Fed up, Annie glared at her sister. "It's not that funny."

"It's very funny," Vivian called out. "Don't tell me you were reading a steamy scene when he appeared?"

"How do you know?" slipped out before Annie could stop herself.

Vivian burst out laughing again.

Heartily exasperated with her sister and the whole situation, Annie stormed out of the kitchen, Vivian's laughter following her all the way to her room.

She only had to get through the next two weeks and make sure she stayed as far away from Craig O'Sullivan as possible. Surely that couldn't be so difficult?

Chapter Three

AUNT JANICE WAITED until they were eating before she began her questioning. Oh so subtly, of course, but Craig had known her most of his life and could tell when she was in her matchmaking mode.

"So, do you think you could help poor Annie with her marketing? I'm really so sorry for her. She's spent a lot of money turning that place into the beautiful house it is now. Of course, Bramble House Bed-and-Breakfast has been operating for much longer and they have loyal guests who wouldn't even think of trying another guesthouse. Annie got some bookings over Valentine's weekend when Bramble House was full, but she needs more. The next two big events in town after next weekend's summer festival are the fair and homecoming, but that's only toward the end of summer. It's important for her to get visitors for next weekend." His aunt was just about out of breath by the time she finally stopped talking.

"She doesn't want my help," he said, helping himself to more of the pork chops his aunt had prepared.

"Of course she'll say that, but isn't part of your job persuading clients to go with your advice?"

Grinning, he looked at her. "Why the sudden interest in Annie Miller's place? Are you trying your matchmaking skills again? I'd thought you'd be happy now that Aiden and Vivian are getting married. You've had a hand in that, haven't you?"

"I may have tried in the past to get you and your cousins to have a little fun, but now that you're all grown up and living your own lives, I don't interfere."

"So, you haven't asked me here for the sole purpose of getting me to talk to Annie about her B and B?"

His aunt looked hurt. "Of course not. Remember, I asked both you and Riley to visit me, not just you. To tell you the truth, I was hoping Riley could make it. She'd be able to take beautiful photographs of Annie and her B and B. Ones Annie could use on her website. I don't know anything about marketing, but even I can see her website is problematic."

"Tell you what—I'll have a look at her website and if … note the *if*," he warned, "she agrees to it, I'll give her some suggestions. Okay?"

His aunt beamed. "That's all I ask. Thank you, dear. Have you heard from your parents lately?"

Craig shrugged. "Last I heard, the team of Doctors Without Borders they've joined was heading to some or other West African country. I haven't heard from them since."

Janice leaned over and patted his hand. "I'm sorry. At times I could shake that brother of mine and his wife. You were so young when they first started leaving you with Sean and Cara. I know they're both doctors, I know they treat and heal people all over the globe, but you were only ten when they've decided to join Doctors Without Borders. Of course, Aiden and Riley were very happy to get a new 'brother,' but it was hard on you."

They'd finished dinner and Craig stood up and began to clear the table. "I found a new home with Aiden and Riley's parents, gaining a brother and sister to boot. I had nothing to complain about."

Aunt Janice cocked her head. "I've often wondered—are your parents the reason you're still single at thirty-six and always dating more than one woman at a time?"

He grinned. "I'm single because I choose to be. I'm always up-front with the women I'm dating. If they know I'm also dating other people, there are no expectations. We have fun until we don't and then we move on."

"Such a pity, though." His aunt smiled. "You'll make such a great husband and dad."

The words *husband* and *dad* exploded in his mind and Craig nearly dropped the plate he was carrying.

"Leave the dishes ..." Aunt Janice began, but he managed to put the plate down without letting it slip to the ground.

Still unsettled, he tried to make light of his reaction.

"Just don't use the m-word again when I'm carrying a plate."

His aunt was grinning as she got up. "Interesting reaction. You won't forget to look at Annie's website?"

"Promise."

WITH A GROAN, Annie sat up and switched on the light on her bedside table. She wasn't going to sleep. The few times she'd managed to drift off, images of beading nipples and Craig's smoldering blue eyes had woken her up.

Seriously, it wasn't as if he was the first attractive man she'd seen since her arrival in Marietta. There were several good-looking men in town and on the ranches scattered around Marietta. In fact, a very sexy cowboy from the Carrigans' ranch, Circle C, had asked her out on a number of occasions, but she'd always had a very legitimate excuse ready. What was his name again? Something to do with animals … Oh, yes, Hunter something.

She'd been wary of dating again. Ted's very harsh message—men weren't interested in women who only wanted to cook and stay in the kitchen—was not something she'd forgotten. But if her body was reacting this way to the first strange man getting close to her, it was maybe time to start dating again.

As long as the word *marriage* wasn't mentioned, she'd be happy to get to know more people in and around Marietta.

Maybe she should message Hunter. He'd gotten hold of her telephone number and had messaged her several times so she had his number.

As she picked up her phone to send a message, it bleeped. She had a text. From Craig.

Of course, he'd have her number, though she hadn't thought he'd ever texted only her. Since Aiden had become part of their family, Vivian had created a family group with all their names.

Warily, she opened the message.

Your website is a mess.

Inhaling sharply, she stared at the small screen. Seriously, she hadn't asked him to help her. Quickly, she jumped out of bed and picked up her laptop from the desk in her room. Her website wasn't a mess, how could he say that? She'd done it herself and was quite proud of her achievement. Okay, she wasn't very techno-savvy, but she'd tried. And yes, it could probably do with some tweaking but a *mess* it certainly wasn't.

She opened her laptop and entered the URL for her website. While she waited for it to open, she looked at Craig's message again. It wasn't that bad and certainly not a mess. Putting down her laptop, she grabbed her phone and typed out a message.

That is harsh.

The two blue marks indicated he'd seen the message. Ha, so he'd been waiting for her reply.

Three dots appeared, disappeared seconds later. Just

when she wanted to switch off her phone again, another messaged appeared.

I could help you.

Ticked off, she quickly messaged back.

Can't afford you, but thanks.

Three dots appeared, disappeared. She waited. Finally, the ping.

You can pay me with one of your meals.

Her fingers hovered over the small keyboard. The payment wasn't the only problem. Before she could message again, her phone bleeped again.

I promise to try and ignore any beading of body parts.

Annie inhaled sharply. She couldn't believe he'd actually written down the word. Her fingers were typing before she'd finished the thought.

And I'll try to ignore the throbbing of body parts.

Only after she'd sent it and the two blue marks appeared, did she register what she'd messaged. Immediately she clicked on the message and deleted it. For everyone. Her phone bleeped.

Too late! I've seen your message. So if we ignore body parts, will you let me help you?

Her fingers were flying over the small keyboard before she could think.

For someone who talks in one-word sentences, your messages are quite lengthy.

She didn't have to wait long.

I talk a lot at work. Do we have a deal?

Sighing, Annie typed her reply.

Dinner tomorrow 7 pm. Anything you don't eat?

Those freaking three dots appeared and disappeared a few times. Finally, she got a reply.

Sounds great, thanks.

Another ping.

Fed up, she closed her phone and switched off the light. Moments later, she groaned out loud. She was smiling and there was definitely beading happening!

THURSDAY EVENING AT seven on the dot, Craig knocked on the door of Annie's B and B. He'd picked up his phone numerous times throughout the day to cancel. At some point, he'd even considered going back to Portland. But here he was, feeling like a schoolboy on his way to pick up his date for the prom.

The door opened, but it wasn't Annie welcoming him. Instead, it was her brother Mitch and the way he was scowling certainly wasn't very welcoming.

"O'Sullivan," he said shortly, putting out his hand.

Craig eyed the big hand warily but there wasn't much else he could do but to shake hands with the big guy. "Hello, Mitch," he got out before his hand was just about crushed.

"I hear there's another Irishman sniffing around one of my sisters and I have to—"

Before Mitch could finish his threat, though, Vivian appeared at his side. "Oh, shush, Mitch. He's here to help

Annie, not woo her. Isn't that right, Craig?" Vivian asked, her eyes twinkling. "Come on in, we're eating in the dining room tonight. Annie has pulled out all the stops. My mouth has been watering since I got back from the hospital today. The smells are divine."

Craig made sure to give Mitch a wide berth. "Is Aiden around?" he asked Vivian trying not to think about the word *woo*. That was so not what he was doing; he'd have to try and put Mitch's mind at rest at some point. He liked Annie's brother, but remembered all too well Mitch was the one who'd punched Aiden.

"He's around, busy on his laptop, chasing a story at the moment, but he should be down in a moment. Mitch, will you get us something to drink?"

Muttering something about Irishmen, Mitch stomped into the house while Craig and Vivian remained at the front door.

Vivian laughed. "Mitch is just being his overprotective self. He's always been a very caring person but ever since Mom and Dad passed away, he's taken it to the next level. Aiden survived his brusque manner, though. I'm sure you will, too."

"I understand why he hasn't welcomed Aiden with open arms. But our situations are different."

"Different how?"

"Aiden wanted you and, well, I don—"

A movement on the steps caught his attention. He

turned just as Annie reached the last step. He didn't remember making a conscious decision to move, but as she reached the final step, he was right in front of her to help her down. His eyes took in everything about her.

She looked gorgeous. Instead of her usual ponytail, her brown hair was loose and hanging down her back, a few strands curling over her shoulder. The wide skirt of the turquoise dress she was wearing ended just above her knee. But it was the nude-colored high heels, making her gorgeous legs look even longer than usual that nearly brought him to his knees. He'd never seen her legs before, she usually wore jeans or pants.

"Annie," he got out, his tongue strangely heavy. "You look … amazing."

He had to have said the correct thing, because she finally smiled at him—one of those big, beautiful smiles that lit up her face.

"You were saying…" Vivian chuckled behind him, but for the life of him he couldn't remember what they'd been talking about.

"So, are we going to eat or not?" Mitch grunted from the kitchen door.

"Yes, we are," Annie said. "Have you opened a bottle of wine, Mitch?"

"Let me get it," Aiden said from behind as he slapped Craig on the shoulder. "Is Mitch giving you the cold shoulder?"

Relieved, Craig grinned. It was good to have his cousin here as well. "I've just arrived."

Annie walked toward the kitchen. "Grab a chair around the dining room table, I'll check on the food."

Aiden leaned closer. "So, how is the hand?" he chuckled.

"Just about crushed," Craig said flexing his fingers.

Mitch frowned and opened his mouth, but Vivian took his arm and steered him away from them before he could say anything.

"What's up with the brother?" Craig asked.

"He feels the same way about his sisters as we feel about Riley. And you ogling Annie isn't helping."

"I'm not ogling Annie. Whatever gave you that idea?"

Aiden laughed. "You're ogling her, whether you want to or not." He sobered, giving Craig a stern look. "I have to mention though, Annie will soon be my sister as well and I know about your two-date rule. Don't mess with her. Having your hand crushed would be the least of your problems then."

This was getting way beyond ridiculous. "I have no idea what you're all going on about. I'm here because Aunt Janice asked me to help Annie with marketing. It's strictly business."

Aiden grinned. "Great. Then we won't have a problem. Come on, I've ordered wine from our favorite Californian cellar for the wedding and also some extra bottles for Annie's guesthouse. There's a very nice cabernet sauvignon …"

They stepped into the big dining room and Craig stopped listening to his cousin. Even though the sun hadn't set yet, Annie was lighting candles on the table. As he watched, she blew out the match she'd used. His body tightened.

What the hell was happening here?

Chapter Four

ANNIE JUST ABOUT leapt out her chair when Mitch finally put down his spoon. She was so glad dinner was finally over. Her brother had been glowering at Craig all through dinner and had hardly said a word. Craig had also been silent and if the slight frown between his eyes was any indication, he was probably wishing he was anywhere but here.

Aiden patted his belly. "Annie, that was sublime. I can honestly say I've never had anything in Portland that comes close to your cooking. Thanks so much." He got up. "You and Craig have a website to discuss, I'll clean up."

"That's not necessary," Annie began, but Vivian pushed her away from the table. "You've been in the kitchen since early this morning. Maybe you and Craig can use your office? I'll bring coffee."

Annie touched her tummy where a flight of butterflies was suddenly coming to life. Alone with the sexy Irishman in her office. *Help.* Vivid images from last night's dreams were running through her mind. So not the time to be thinking about those, seriously.

It was the reason why Craig was here, though, she couldn't postpone being alone with him a moment longer.

"Craig, this way?" She vaguely smiled in his direction before she marched toward her office. There was a small coffee table and a couch, they could work there.

Annie only realized her dilemma as Craig closed the door of her office behind him. It was a small room. More than spacious enough for her, but with the big Irishman in it, the space seemed to have miraculously shrunk to the size of a doll's house.

"Um, you can sit on the couch. I'll join you in a moment. I just want to get a pen and pad and my laptop."

"I have to agree with Aiden about your food. I can't remember when last I had meal this good. You're an amazing cook."

"Thank you," she murmured while rummaging through the drawers of her desk. In an effort to find her equilibrium, she was taking deep breaths but probably overdid it, because by the time she had the pad and pen in her hands, she was light-headed.

"Seriously, Annie," she muttered to herself as she moved to join Craig.

Oh, my goodness. Had the couch always been this small?

As Annie took the other seat next to Craig, the subtle

flowery and citrusy scent he'd come to associate with her wafted over him, slipped through every pore on his skin until he was just about breathing her in.

It had been a struggle not staring openly at her all night. When feeding people, she relaxed, exuding a warmth that simply reeled in everyone around her table. She made sure everyone else was eating before she helped herself. A true nurturer, she was happy when those around her were happy.

As she leaned forward to open her laptop, the shoulder of the top of her dress slid down her arm, revealing the thin satiny strap of a midnight-black bra. She readjusted the strap, but the damage was done, his body didn't need much more to react.

Ignore the body parts—that had been the deal.

Restlessly, he moved on the seat, trying to find a comfortable position that would hide his reaction from Annie.

"Okay, here we are," Annie finally said. "I don't think it looks that bad." She glanced at him over her shoulder, the movement bringing her even closer to him. Her soft lips were about an inch from his.

Clearly startled, she jumped up and started pacing. "Okay, so tell me. What is wrong with my website and what can I do that won't cost me a fortune?"

Craig forced himself to pick up the laptop. Apart from the fact that it would hide his very obvious reaction to Annie, it would hopefully help him to focus on the reason he was here.

Clearing his throat, he used the few seconds to try and gather his thoughts. "Well, the first problem is that when I've searched for *B and B in Marietta* or *guesthouse in Marietta* on any search engine on the internet, there is no mention of Annie's. So, the noticeable problem seems to be that you don't rank high on the search engine results pages. There are ways you can improve your SEO ratings, like incorporating keywords into your page titles, meta descriptions, and content. Also, your website isn't optimized for mobile platforms, a significant factor in the ranking algorithm. Your page also loads very slowly, something that prevents you from earning high rankings."

Annie had stopped pacing and was looking dumbstruck. "I have absolutely no idea what you've just said. What on earth is SEO and the meta what-what you've mentioned?"

His first instinct was to pick her up and tell her everything would be okay, he'd do it for her, but he doubted that would be well received. Annie was no shrinking violet.

He handed her pad to her. "I'll talk, you write. We also have to get Riley here as quickly as possible. You need photos. Lots and lots of them."

Taking the pad from him, she sat down next to him again. "There are beautiful photos on my website," she cried out.

"You're right. Beautiful photos. Of the town, of the mountain—all good and well, but there is nothing that distinguishes you from any other B and B."

"I don't understand."

He put his hand on her chest, just above her breasts. It was an instinctive gesture, one he often used, but when his hand touched the skin above the line of her dress, he had to inhale before he could continue.

Annie's eyes widened and she quickly grabbed hold of his hand. Lacing his fingers with hers, he kept his hand against her chest.

"What makes this B and B different to any other place I've ever been to is you, Annie. You're the brand you want to sell. To only have photos of the house and the luxury rooms, lovely as they are, is not enough. You are selling much more than just a building or rooms. What you're selling, is *your* B and B and that's what you should focus on. Photos of you welcoming guests, photos of you in the kitchen, in the dining room, your food…" He grinned. "Of you reading in your hammock—those are the images that would get visitors to want to come to Annie's." The last word was a mere whisper.

Had he moved forward or had she? He had no idea. Her brown eyes nearly liquid chocolate, she gasped softly, her lips parted.

Fascinated, he pulled her slowly closer. "I want to kiss you, Annie …"

"Maybe not a good idea," she got out. "Some of my body parts are not behaving."

His eyes dropped. "I can see that. Mine is not behaving

either." He chuckled as he slipped a hand beneath her hair. "Just one kiss?" he asked, teasing her lips. "Surely our body parts can handle that?"

"Okay, but just one." She sighed and met his lips.

It was only going to be a meeting of lips, a taste to find out whether her mouth was as soft as it looked, but the moment their lips met, a strange current flickered through his body, making a particular body part misbehave even more.

Trying desperately to rein in his galloping libido, Craig tried not to succumb to the hunger heating his blood within seconds. A soft moan escaped from Annie's throat, though, her lips opened up, and he was lost. His tongue shot forward, meeting her dancing one. In that instant, he could swear the earth shifted beneath his feet.

As he pulled her even closer, her leg slipped over his lap pushing the laptop to slide from his lap. It fell soundlessly to the floor. Fortunately, there was a carpet, was his last rational thought before his senses took over.

ANNIE WAS LOST in a sea of feeling and emotions. Craig's lips and tongue were taking her to heights of pleasure she'd never experienced before. She had to stop him. Hadn't they agreed to ignore their misbehaving body parts? Oh, but she hadn't yet had enough, not nearly enough. She loved the feeling of the stubble of his beard against her face, the heat of his big hand around her breast, and the heady scent of leather mixed with vanilla and suede surrounding them.

A hoarse little voice finally penetrated her bemused mind—*his hand around her breast.*

Pushing him away, she gulped in much-needed air. No wonder she'd nearly landed on Craig's lap—she was just about deprived of oxygen. "We said kiss, not touching …" she croaked. Her hand covered his. "This is way beyond kissing …"

There was a knock on the door. "Annie? Coffee?" It was Vivian.

Craig exhaled slowly, his eyes never leaving hers. "Damn Annie, you're killing me…" His voice was a mere whisper.

Delicious chills ran down her spine. Nobody had ever looked at her like that. She'd always thought only heroes in romance novels used that line, not real life heroes as well.

"Annie?" Vivian called again. "Everybody decent?"

The door opened just as Craig quickly picked up the laptop and placed it back on his lap—but not before Annie caught a glimpse of the clear indication of his desire.

Their eyes met. His eyes dropped to her chest, the one corner of his mouth lifting slightly.

Crossing her arms in the hope of concealing her freaking beading breasts, Annie turned to smile as Vivian put the tray down on the coffee table in front of them. "Thanks, sis. Craig …" She had to clear her throat before she could continue. "Has some good ideas."

Vivian kept her face straight, but her eyes were sparkling. "I never doubted that for a moment. Thank you, Craig. Annie certainly does need … help."

Annie glared at Vivian, but her sister ignored her scowl. "We're going up to our room—see you tomorrow!" she sang as she left.

The door closed behind Vivian.

ANNIE JUMPED UP and began pacing again, sending him furtive glances at every turn.

Rubbing his face, he swallowed a groan. Thank goodness for Vivian's interruption. It had supposed to have been a quick kiss. He had to taste her… And now that he had, all he could think about was kissing her again.

Finally, Annie stopped and leaned against the desk. "That cannot happen again."

He nodded. "I agree." He picked up the pad and pen. "I suggest you sit behind your desk…"

She stepped forward and took the items from him. Their fingers met, desire reared its head again. This time he couldn't stop the groan. "You'll be the death of me, woman. Go sit over there where I can't touch you or smell you or…"

Annie's eyes darkened and his eyes dropped to the clear outline of her nipples pushing against the top of her dress as they did when she was turned on—by now, he knew the signs.

She quickly turned away and took a seat behind the desk.

Inhaling deeply, he opened the laptop again. *Focus O'Sullivan, focus. You're here to help. She's a client like any other client.* "As I've said, you, Annie, are the brand you need to sell to prospective visitors. And we can do that by first of all improving your SEO ratings…"

"Okay, what is that?"

He steadily kept his eyes on the computer. If he didn't look at her, maybe the temptation to get up and go and kiss her again might just fade. "It stands for search engine optimization. It's the process of taking steps to help a website or piece of content rank higher on a search engine, for example, Google."

Groaning, she dropped her head in hands. "I still have no idea what you're talking about."

He smiled. Annie always had that effect on him. "If someone is looking for a B and B or guesthouse in and around Marietta, you want Annie's to be right at the top of the list that would be generated when someone searches for guesthouses or a B and B online. The two core elements of SEO are the on-page SEO and the off-page SEO. The on-page SEO is about building content to improve your ranking. This comes down to incorporating…"

It was going quite well, but then he made the mistake of looking up at Annie. His eyes seemed to have a will of their own. She wasn't making any notes, she was staring at him.

"Annie…"

She started scribbling furiously. "Okay, SEO, got it. What else?"

"You haven't heard a word I've said."

Still scribbling, she didn't look up. "Of course, I've heard."

"What have I said?"

"Uh … something about branding?"

"That was before the kiss. When I touched you."

Sighing, she dropped the pen and looked at him. "Maybe we should take a break. Try doing this during daylight hours. We've had wine, I haven't dated in a while, you're attractive and … well, the romances I've been reading… Maybe I should try reading some murder mysteries for a while. At least until you're gone."

With his eyes on Annie, Craig put the laptop on the coffee table in front of him and slowly got up. "Let me get this straight—you think if we work together during the day and not drink wine, we won't want to kiss?"

"I should also date more. And not read about beading breasts…" She closed her eyes. "I can't believe I've said that out loud again! You do this to me." She scowled as she jumped up. "Come on, I'll see you out."

He moved toward the door and waited for her. They both reached for the knob, his hand closed around hers. "Tell you what—today is Thursday. I'll come around

Saturday morning. You date and read a murder mystery and we'll see how it goes. Oh, and don't drink wine. Meanwhile, I'll see what I can do about your website. Text me your password. There are a few things I can try before we have new pictures. I'll also make sure when Riley will arrive so that she could take some photographs…"

He lost his train of thought, his words. Annie's eyes had dropped to his lips and *would you look at that*? His hand slipped around her neck. "Damn it, Annie. Do you have any idea what all the beading is doing to me?" Bringing her close to him, his lips trailed down her face while his hand teased one of her hardened nipples.

"You mean the throbbing? Oh, yeah, I can feel it." She sighed.

It took him a heartbeat to know what she was referring to. Grinning, he pulled her even closer. "You're funny, Annie Miller. And so beautiful, I can't stop staring at you."

Surprised, she shook her head. "I'm the plain one. Vivian is the one who turns heads."

His mouth had found the soft spot just below her ear. "What idiot has told you that?"

"The one who called off our wedding weeks before the date."

He lifted his head. "Is he the reason you're not dating?"

Staring at him, she chewed on her lower lip. The simple gesture had been all he'd been thinking about over the last couple of months. And now he knew exactly how sweet she tasted. He simply had to taste her again.

"I don't mind dating. I just don't want to do the wedding thing again. Being dumped kinda put me off marriage for good."

His smile grew bigger. "Really? Well, in that case, I may have a proposition for you."

Warily, she looked up at him. "What kind of proposition?"

"We'll talk on Saturday. After your date and murder mystery."

"I don't think—"

"Don't"—he chuckled as he lowered his head again—"think. Tonight, we feel."

With desire clawing at his throat, he captured her lips with his, swallowing her sigh. Within minutes, he was lost in a sea of sensation and feelings, the only voice he could hear, the one egging him on to never stop.

ANNIE CLUNG TO Craig, trying her best to ignore the pesky little voice shouting hoarsely all sorts of warnings. When he walked out of the door tonight, this would never happen again. Just another minute…

Craig's restless hands moved up and down her body, lighting little fires on the surface of her skin wherever he touched her. When his hand slipped beneath her dress and stroked her leg, she was ready to burst into flames.

"You have gorgeous legs, have I told you?" he whispered against her mouth.

But she didn't want to talk. Talking forced her to think and she wasn't ready to do that yet.

Craig's hand slowly slid higher up her leg, inch by torturing inch. By the time he was close to her heat, she was just about burning up.

"Craig…" slipped out.

Cussing softly, Craig removed his hand from under her dress and cupped her face. His blue eyes were stormy. "I should go."

Neither of them moved away. "Yeah, you should."

"One more kiss?"

"I don't think…" she began but he was already bending his head. "No hands, promise." And dropping his hands to his sides, he proceeded to kiss her senseless, yet again.

By the time he finally lifted his head, they were both breathing heavily.

"Saturday?" he asked.

Unable to speak, she put out a hand to steady herself against the wall and nodded.

Taking her hand, he opened the door. "Walk me to the front door?"

Threading his fingers through hers, they silently walked toward the front door.

Craig opened it. "Don't come out, it's cold. Saturday?

What time?"

"Eleven?"

He nodded and lifting their hands, pressed a kiss on hers before he quickly walked out on to the porch. He stopped and turned, half a smile on his face. "The sexy Irishman you were talking about when I found you in your hammock—is it me?"

"What do you think?"

Exhaling slowly, he gave her one of his killer smiles. "I had to make sure." With a small wave, he jogged down the stairs to his car.

Annie watched him until the taillights disappeared. Only then did she closed the door, dropping her forehead against the wood.

If she wasn't mistaken, she was in deep trouble.

WHEN SHE FINALLY got into bed half an hour later, her phone bleeped. It was Craig.

Remember details for website.

While she was reading this, another message popped up.

Thanks for the meal.

Seconds later, another one.

I like kissing you.

She quickly sent him the login details for her website. Three dots appeared, disappeared. Finally, another message appeared.

Nothing else?

Groaning out loud, she stared at the small screen. What would happen if she were to message him all the confusing thoughts running through her mind? *I love kissing you, I love being in your arms, I love spending time with you, you make me smile, you make me ... happy.* Here she was, grinning like a fool.

Ditto

Three dots appeared, disappeared. Nothing. Just as she was putting her phone down, it bleeped again.

Minutes later, she was lying down, staring wide-eyed at the ceiling, a stupid grin on her face. She wasn't going to sleep a wink tonight.

Chapter Five

CRAIG WAS WORKING on his computer in the kitchen late Friday afternoon when Janice rushed in, out of breath. "Craig, sweetie, it's so nice to have you here. I was just wondering, why don't we go out to dinner? Marietta is, of course, not the city, but we do have a few places serving lovely food."

Getting up, he stretched. "Good idea. I've been sitting here since this morning."

"Aren't you supposed to be taking a break?"

Grinning, he nodded. "Yeah, but then someone suggested I help a certain B and B owner with her marketing."

Aunt Janice grinned. "So, is that what you've been doing? Helping Annie? But shouldn't you ... I don't know, be with her when you do that?"

"We spoke last night and I'll see her tomorrow. She's sent me the details I needed to get into her website; I've been working on that today. Hopefully, Riley will be able to arrive a few days before the wedding so she could take a few pictures in and around the guesthouse. There is so much more she could do but if we can at least help to get more visitors to her website, she should be halfway there."

"I'm so glad to hear you're helping her. Annie is such a special person and her cooking! You should know after last night."

"Oh, yes, she's one of a kind indeed," he murmured.

"Interesting." Aunt Janice grinned.

"What do you mean?"

She'd turned around and was walking out of the kitchen. "You haven't said anything about her cooking." Grinning over her shoulder, she left the kitchen.

Craig stared after his aunt, his thoughts back with Annie. She was all he'd been thinking about since this morning. He'd had emails from work, calls from clients, a few frantic messages from his team, but throughout, she'd always been somewhere in the recesses of his mind.

Countless times during the day, he'd picked up his phone to call or message her. In fact, at some point he'd actually written a whole message, asking her not to date anyone else, before he'd deleted it.

He couldn't forget her scent, her smile, the way she chewed her lip, the way her eyes darkened when they'd kissed, the satiny texture of her long, slender legs…

Cussing softly, he picked up his laptop and made his way to his room. She wasn't even in the same room as him and his body parts were misbehaving. Surely, the small town of Marietta would have some other females he could get to know in the next two weeks? Maybe that was the problem—

he wasn't used to not dating or having sex. Come to think of it, he couldn't even remember the last time he'd dated anyone?

Frowning, he stared out of the window of his room, not really seeing anything. It couldn't be since he'd been here, could it? His thoughts racing, he tried to recall his last date. It had been before he and Riley had decided to join Aiden in Marietta. So that meant he hadn't dated anyone since he'd been here about two months ago. Since he'd met Annie. Surely, that couldn't be the reason, could it?

Unbuttoning his shirt, he walked toward the bathroom. But, okay, he'd been busy at work, there had been the mad rush to make sure they impressed the client with the new coffee brand more than their competitors and the whole sordid aftermath after their triumph. There hadn't really been time and, to be honest, there wasn't anyone special he'd cared to be with.

He stilled before he stepped into the shower. A cold one. Leaning with his arms against the tiles, he waited for the water to cool down his body.

Minutes later, he closed the tap. Apparently not even a cold shower during the end of winter could keep his blood from heating when thoughts of Miss Annie Miller intruded.

NERVOUSLY, ANNIE PACED the hallway. It was just before

half past seven and she was dressed and ready for her date with Hunter. In the end, it hadn't been necessary for her to message him, she'd run into the tall, lanky cowboy in town while in the pharmacy.

Like always, he'd grinned and suggested dinner and was dumbstruck for a few minutes after she'd agreed. But she had a date with him and hopefully his nearness would also lead to some beading of her body parts—she desperately needed to know whether her reaction to Craig was because simply she hadn't dated for a while or whether he was the only man who had that effect on her.

Fortunately, Vivian had left for the hospital early this morning and Annie was dressing when she'd arrived earlier. She also hadn't seen Mitch and he wasn't back from school yet.

This was why she was waiting here, at the front door. She wanted to be gone before either Vivian or Mitch saw her. Her sister would have questions about last night, probably Mitch as well, and Annie really didn't want to talk about it.

She'd been chastising herself all day. Craig and she had been supposed to work and from the little she'd understood from what he'd said, it was clear he knew what he was talking about. But what had she done? Like a sex-starved spinster, she'd just about jumped his bones. After another night of dreaming about her beading nipples and Craig's deep blue eyes and warm hands, she was determined to enjoy her date.

A sound on her right made Annie look up.

Vivian was coming down the stairs.

Ugh.

Vivian grinned. "I hear you have a date with Hunter Grant?"

"How on earth do you know that?" Annie exclaimed.

"Well, let me see. Carol Bingley told..."

Annie held up her hand. "I don't want to know! I suppose by now everyone in town will know."

"Even Craig, I'm sure." Vivian chuckled. "After last night, I honestly thought your first date in Marietta would be with him. The two of you looked awfully cozy on the couch."

"He was giving me tips to improve my website. Your suggestion, remember?"

"If you say so. But if I'm not mistaken, you had the look of someone who has just been thoroughly kissed. Am I wrong?"

"It was ... nothing. Just a kiss..."

"I knew it!" Vivian grinned. "So that's why you've suddenly agreed to go on a date with Hunter."

"I've read a murder mystery and I'm dating someone else," Annie said.

She didn't have to tell Vivian the book she'd read actually had many more love scenes in it than any romance she'd read. Maybe she should try science fiction. Robots or spaceships with green or blue aliens surely wouldn't turn her on, would it?

Vivian chuckled. "My dear sister, you do have it bad, don't you? Murder mystery? I assume you're going on a date with Hunter because you're hoping you'll have the same response to his kisses that you had when Craig kissed you, but what does reading mystery novels have to do with the whole thing?"

Fortunately, a knock on the front door saved Annie from having to answer her sister.

"Hi, Hunter." Annie smiled as she opened the door.

The tall cowboy returned her smile. "Annie. You look lovely."

"Thank you."

"How's the arm?" Vivian asked as she stepped closer.

"Fine, Doc—thanks to you."

"I'm ready," Annie said. Hopefully, she and Hunter could leave before Mitch arrived.

"After you." Hunter smiled and held the door for Annie. "Night, Doc."

"Enjoy your evening!" Vivian called after them, clearly highly amused.

BY HALF PAST seven, Craig and Aunt Janice were seated at a table in Rocco's Restaurant. It wasn't difficult to decide what to eat—pizza seemed to be the big thing on the menu. The Tuscan landscapes covering the faux plaster walls and the red-and-white checked cloths were clearly meant to create an Italian look.

They placed their order of pizza and some chianti on Aunt Janice's insistence. A few more customers entered, all greeting Aunt Janice and asking to be introduced to him. The waiter brought the bottle of wine.

"You seem to be happy here, Aunt Janice." He smiled and lifted his glass.

His aunt nodded. "I am. When you all left home and started your own lives, I knew it was time for me to let you go. It's not that easy, though, and I'd hoped moving far away would give you all enough breathing space. I've missed you all terribly, though. I was so glad when Aiden finally accepted my invitation to come and visit. And here you are as well."

"And now Aiden is getting married and settling down in Marietta." Craig chuckled. "Close to you."

"I couldn't be happier."

"You do know none of us minded having you close by. You were there when we needed you most. We'll never forget that. The way you stepped in when first Aiden and Riley's dad passed and then their mom ... we owe you big-time."

"You were the one who kept Aiden and Riley going. You were there when Riley was left at the altar..."

"We both were. I still feel I should've voiced my concerns about the idiot she'd wanted to marry sooner."

"Things happen for a reason. You know how firmly I believe that. There are better things waiting for both you and Riley—if, of course, you have the courage to grab all the chances you get with both hands. But I want to talk about you, Craig. For so long, you've been looking out for Aiden and Riley, but what about you? You have to make time for love, sweetheart. You think there is time, but there isn't, trust me, I know."

He was about to ask his aunt what she meant when a movement from the door had him turn his head. And there she was. Annie. The woman he'd been dreaming about last night and who had been on his mind the whole day. He was getting ready to stand up to greet her when he noticed the tall guy with her. Her date. Of course. Hadn't he been the one who'd told her to go on a date?

The man had his hand at Annie's back and was laughing down at her.

"Craig?" Aunt Janice asked, putting a hand on his arm. "Are you okay? You look ready to explode."

Inhaling deeply, he forced himself to look at his aunt. "I'm fine."

"Something has upset you…" She turned her head just as Annie and her date passed their table.

Annie faltered and stopped as she saw him. Wide brown eyes met his before she turned to this aunt. "Janice! So nice to see you."

Craig stood up.

"Hi, Annie," his aunt said. "I didn't know you and Hunter were dating. Hi, Hunter. You should hold on to this one—she cooks like an angel."

Hunter took Annie's elbow. "I intend to."

"No, we're not dating," Annie interjected. "We're having dinner. Um … Hunter, this is Craig O'Sullivan, Janice's godson. Craig, Hunter Grant."

Craig wasn't even going to acknowledge the guy who was all over Annie, but when the man smiled and held out his hand, he had no choice but to greet him. Hunter managed not to wince, but the glint in his eye confirmed he'd received the not so subtle message Craig had conveyed with a very firm shake.

"Enjoy your dinner, excuse us," Hunter said, taking Annie's hand as they walked away.

"Uh … Craig? Everything okay?" his aunt asked.

Only then he realized he was still standing. For the first time, he also became aware of the curious glances from the other patrons. Quickly, he sat down.

His aunt chuckled. "The woman sitting at the table to your right is Carol Bingley, the town gossip. I bet you before midnight, the whole town will know about you and Hunter Grant fighting over Annie."

"I wasn't fighting over Annie." He scowled, only realizing how loudly he'd spoken when a few heads turned their way.

His aunt lifted her glass, eyes twinkling. "No? Well, from where I sat, I'd say the lines were drawn."

Craig tried to breathe but a band had tightened around his chest and getting enough oxygen into his lungs was difficult.

Chapter Six

HUNTER WAS TALKING but there was such a loud noise in Annie's ears, she couldn't hear what he was saying. Why in the world would Craig pick the same restaurant and same time to eat at Rocco's Italian restaurant? Had he heard about her date with Hunter?

The waiter arrived and Annie forced herself to focus on the menu. She was trying to read the words in front of her, but the letters kept moving around, making it difficult to understand anything.

"Annie?" Hunter asked. "Shall I order a bottle of wine? What do you prefer?"

"Why don't you order?" she smiled.

"Beer?" he asked.

She hated beer, but she smiled and nodded. Hunter was a very nice guy, attractive, attentive, everything she liked and admired in a man but ... since he'd picked her up, there hadn't been the remotest sign of beading anywhere on her body.

He was obviously a tactile person and kept finding ways to touch her, and although it was very sweet and felt nice to be admired, her hormones were unimpressed.

Her eyes kept straying to the table where Craig and Janice were enjoying their meal. Janice was sitting with her back toward them, but Craig was facing her and the table where Annie and Hunter were sitting. When next her eyes turned their way, he was taking a sip of his wine. A pair of dark blue eyes met hers.

The waiter was back with their beers.

"What would you like to order?" Hunter asked.

"What do you recommend?" she asked the waiter. She wasn't even going to try and read the food menu, there was no way she could focus on words at the moment.

The waiter explained about pizza and when she heard *bacon and cheese*, she nodded. "That sounds great, thank you."

Smiling, Hunter handed the menus to the waiter. "Make that two. A woman after my own heart."

As the waiter moved away, he picked up Annie's hand. "You want to tell me why Janice's godson was ready to slug me?" Bringing her hand up to his mouth, Hunter kissed her hand.

A lovely gesture, but not even one lost butterfly was tempted to flutter in her tummy. She looked up. Craig's blue eyes were mere slits, focused on her hand in Hunter's.

"Craig? His cousin is marrying my sister, we're practically family." She smiled. "He's just used to playing the role of older brother. If you are worried about him, you should steer clear of Mitch."

Hunter chuckled. "Believe me, I know. I've heard what he's done to Aiden. But your sister is getting married to the guy, so…" He grinned.

Annie laughed. He really was a very nice man.

BY THE TIME he'd paid for dinner, Craig was ready to put his fist down Hunter's throat. The man hadn't dropped Annie's hand once during dinner. How the hell was she supposed to eat?

Aunt Janice took his arm. "Are you ready to leave?" she asked.

Only then did he realize he was still glaring at Annie's date. Muttering beneath his breath, he stomped out of the restaurant. Behind him, his aunt stopped to greet people, but he didn't stop. He couldn't talk to anyone at the moment.

Walking toward his car, he inhaled the crisp, cold air. What the hell was wrong with him? Who Annie dated was none of his business. Even if her date wanted to take her home, kiss her, and take her to his bed, it was still none of his business. He shouldn't care, it shouldn't bother him. He was here for two weeks.

Still waving at someone behind her, his aunt approached his car. "Thank you so much, I had a lovely time."

Craig opened the door for her, his eyes straying toward

the entrance of Rocco's Italian Restaurant. Just then Annie and her date stepped outside. The guy was holding Annie's elbow, smiling down at her, clearly also captivated.

A band tightened around his chest, making breathing difficult.

"Everything okay, Craig?" his aunt asked.

He was still staring at Annie and her date, damn it. He closed his aunt's door and walked around to get into the car.

He was hoping for a silent drive home, but his aunt had a lot to say. "I'm so happy for Annie that she's finally said yes to Hunter. He works on the Circle C, one of their trusted hands. A seriously nice guy with, according to Carol Bingley, a ranch in Colorado waiting for him. I can see Annie on a ranch—she'd love it there."

He grunted. There wasn't anything else to say. His aunt was right—living on a ranch would suit Annie perfectly. She deserved happiness after that idiot had dumped her, the same one who'd also managed to let Annie doubt herself.

"Thanks, Craig, it was lovely having my very attractive godson escorting me to dinner."

Craig looked down at his aunt. He'd driven home, parked the car but couldn't remember doing any of it. His mind had been full of Annie.

"What about a hot chocolate?" his aunt asked.

"Not for me, thanks," he said as he got out of the car. "I'm not tired yet, I'm going for a walk."

Aunt Janice looked up at the sky. "Don't forget to look

at the stars. They're one of the reasons I could never live in the city again. With all the city lights, one never gets to see the stars. And you have a crescent moon to boot. I'm going to bed, you have a key?"

"I have. See you later." He waited until his aunt had closed the door behind her, before he strolled away. The house was going to be too small for him tonight. Maybe a walk would clear his head and cool his blood.

ANNIE QUICKLY CLOSED the door behind her. Hunter had kissed her and she'd really tried her best to return his kiss as enthusiastically as she'd kissed Craig. Hunter was so good-looking, he smelled nice, and he really knew how to kiss so … She looked down at herself. No beading. No butterflies in her tummy, no rushing of blood, no silly hormones at play, nothing.

Frowning, she began to take off her jacket but stopped. Maybe the fresh air would do her good. It had just turned half past nine, it wasn't that late.

Opening and closing the door softly behind her, she stepped out on to the porch, pulling her jacket closer around her. It was still cold this time of night, but she couldn't face her room just yet.

With her hands in her pockets, she walked down the street. In most of the houses, the lights were still on. People were going about their ordinary lives. A car started close by, someone laughed, a baby cried.

Babies. She'd always loved babies and had been looking forward to having her own someday. That dream had died with Ted's cruel message weeks before their wedding. She'd been happy and content up till now, though. Then two things had happened. First, the guests she'd been so sure would arrive once she'd opened her doors hadn't appeared, and two, Craig O'Sullivan, the person who could potentially help her to change that, had her so confused she'd kissed him.

At least she now knew one thing for sure—Craig was the only man who could turn her legs to rubber with just a look, who had the ability to get the beading going, who could kiss her senseless and make her feel things she'd never felt before.

"Talking to yourself again?" a voice asked.

Annie stopped and blinked. Craig was standing right in front of her. "What are you doing here?"

"I needed fresh air."

"Me, too."

"Have you read your mystery novel?"

She nodded.

"And?"

"Maybe science fiction will work better."

He chuckled softly, his breath caressing her cheek.

"Did he kiss you?"

She inhaled sharply. "You can't ask me that!" she cried

out softly.

Craig took a step closer.

The butterflies in her tummy went ballistic.

"You wanted to test your theory," he said. "I'm in on the deal, so of course I have to know if your experiment worked."

"Yes, he kissed me. And it was … it was … nice."

"Any beading?" In the dim glow of the streetlight, his eyes looked feverish.

Her body responded. "No, damn it," she grumbled.

His fingers grazed her nipples. "It's beading now. Why is that, do you think?"

Mesmerized, she watched his mouth, her own just about dribbling.

The hysterical little voice finally penetrated the red haze of desire and shakily, she took a step back. "It doesn't count. I had wine."

He chuckled. "Okay. So one out of the three. We'll test your theory tomorrow in the light of day when we're both stone-cold sober. Let me walk you home." He took her hand.

Silently, they walked down the street toward her house. With every step, she grew more and more aware of him. They didn't have far to walk, but by the time they'd reached the front door of her house, she was feverish with need.

Quickly, she took the key from her pocket and tried to unlock the door. It fell. They both crouched down to pick it up. Their hands touched.

Craig groaned as he stood up. "Damn, Annie, you'll be the death of me."

He took the key and unlocked the door. "I'll see you around ten?"

She had to brush against him to enter her house. His warm breath caressed her face. She had one more step to take, but then she made the mistake of looking up at him.

He cupped her face. "Just one kiss?"

"Okay, but no hands," she breathed.

Dropping his hands, he chuckled. "You drive a hard bargain, Miss Annie." He bent his head and warm, urgent lips captured hers. A whirlwind picked her up, her senses took over her brain and with a moan, she grabbed hold of his shirt with both her hands.

Hungrily, his mouth moved over her face, trailing wet kisses down her neck, before his lips met hers again. Big hands slid down her back, molding her against him. She reveled in his hardness, the ache that had settled deep in her belly became almost unbearable.

"Annie? Is that you?" Mitch called from somewhere in the house.

Annie lifted her head, her breath coming out in gasps. With her eyes on Craig, she inhaled deeply. "Yeah, it's me!" she called, grateful her voice was working.

"You'd better go," she said.

He looked down. "You said no hands."

Quickly she dropped her arms. "I ... you ... sorry."

His smiled nearly buckled her knees. "I'm not. I like kissing you. I like your hands on me. I like my hands on you..." And without taking his eyes from her, he cupped one of her breasts.

"Craig..." she got out.

From above, they heard footsteps approaching the top of the stairs and she just about pushed Craig out of the door.

Craig stepped outside and she began closing the door.

"I'll see you tomorrow. Dream of me?" Craig asked.

Still trying to catch her breath, she frowned. "That's part of the problem. I have these X-rated dreams with you in them..."

"Annie?" Mitch asked, much closer now and she quickly closed the door.

"Was that the cowboy?"

"We had a very nice dinner," Annie said. Not quite answering Mitch's question wasn't lying.

"I'm glad. I'd like to meet him next time."

She shrugged. "I don't think there'll be a next time."

"Oh? Any particular reason? Or should I ask—any particular other person?"

Brushing past him, she took the stairs two at a time to the upper level. "Good night, Mitch."

"Tell that Irishman I'm watching him!" Mitch called out as she disappeared into her room.

She dearly loved her siblings and adored her brother, but

seriously, he didn't have to be quite so … so… With a sigh, she sat on her bad. Caring was the word she was looking for. And she loved the fact that Mitch cared enough.

Her phone bleeped. A text from Craig. Her heart flipped, her blood heated, the butterflies moved. Pressing her hand against her tummy, she picked up her phone and opened the message.

Any particular X-rated dream you'd cared to share?

Her body still humming, Annie sent a text.

CRAIG SAT ON his bed, staring at his phone. He'd jogged the short distance back to his aunt's house. He was on fire for Annie and definitely needed a cold shower. Telling him she was having X-rated dreams about him—how was he supposed to sleep knowing that?

He loved the way Annie blurted out her feelings. She was a straight shooter, no coy innuendos, she told it like it was. What was happening between them was clearly as inconvenient for her as it was for him, but she didn't hold back, told him what he made her feel. And that… Inhaling deeply, he chuckled. That was just about the sexiest thing about her. Except for those legs that seemed to go on forever or her generous, soft breasts, beading in anticipation of his touch.

Shifting on the bed, he cussed softly. Damn, he wasn't even near the woman and she was making him all hot and bothered.

His phone bleeped.

Midnight-black sheets…

The words conjured up an immediate picture of Annie's long legs flung over him, a black silk sheet covering her body.

Inhaling raggedly, he texted her back. *We're naked?*

Three dots appeared, disappeared again. Finally, his phone bleeped again.

Indeed.

He had to laugh. The prim word thrown in after their flirtatious bantering, was hilarious.

Still grinning, he texted. *See you tomorrow.*

Within seconds he had an answer. *No wine, remember?*

Chuckling, he sent her an emoji.

By the time he'd showered and climbed into bed, he was still smiling. Minutes later, he had to kick off the blankets. Damn, vivid scenes of naked bodies on midnight-black sheets were running through his mind already and he hadn't even fallen asleep.

Chapter Seven

T HE FIRST BATCH of scones burned. Dumbstruck, Annie stared at the nearly charcoal-colored round blobs on the tray she'd grabbed out of the oven. This had never happened to her before!

Muttering, she opened the trashcan and dropped the humiliation in it before Mitch or Vivian could witness the mess.

Of course, she hadn't been able to fall asleep last night. What she'd tried instead was reading a science-fiction story. After several searches, she'd downloaded a book of Ursula K. Le Guin, a famous science-fiction author. The book she'd picked was apparently one of the author's earlier works—the coming of age of a young wizard.

The story was brilliantly written and actually kept her interested but... One would think reading about mages and wizards summoning beasts would fill her mind with the wonder of other realities, but no, she'd ended up dreaming again about Craig O'Sullivan and his searing kisses. Every time she'd closed her eyes, there he was with his killer smile, sexy body, and dark blue eyes.

Dropping the burnt tray onto the kitchen counter, she again began to measure out the flour and baking powder. Whisking the eggs for the next batch, she tried to focus on the task at hand, but of course, after only a few seconds her thoughts began to stray again.

Those freaking lines from the romance novel she'd been reading, when Craig had found her in the hammock, seemed to be forever stuck in her head, intruding at the most inconvenient times.

The beading of nipples—there had to be another way to describe this particular reaction, surely?—heroes *shuddering*, and *talking hoarsely*. She'd always smiled when reading this, it was just a fantasy, not something that happened in real life, surely?

And then Craig had kissed her, had touched her, and what had happened? Nipples beaded and not only did the hero shudder, the heroine was definitely also doing some shaking and trembling herself. Not to forget the talking hoarsely and oh, the *you're killing me* while he was looking at her as if he'd wanted to pick her up and take her to his cave or wherever heroes took the women they fell for.

Fell for? Where did that come from? Nobody was falling for anybody, damn it. The whisk slid out of her hand, toppled the bowl in which she was mixing the ingredients and the gooey, yellow batter ran over her legs, covering her feet.

"Se-rious-ly!" she cried out. "I can do this in my sleep,

what's wrong with me?"

Vivian appeared in the kitchen door. Annie felt like crying. Of course, her sister would pick this exact moment to step into the kitchen. It wasn't any fun to make a mess without anyone to witness it.

"Annie?" Vivian rushed closer and took in the mess with one glance. "What happened?"

"I am burning the lot of them!" Annie growled looking down at her feet covered in the mixture for the scones. "Every single one."

Vivian sniffed in the air. "It smells as if something has already been burnt—what else do you want to burn? And why are you up so early? It's Saturday."

"It's those freaking romances I've been reading. They're the reason for this mess and why I've burned scones. Burnt scones! Who does that? I've certainly never burned anything before in my life. But those books are ridiculous and make me do and dream..." Annie caught her breath. As usual, there was no stopping her thoughts running out of her mouth.

Vivian lifted an eyebrow. "Anything I should know? Is it really the romances or could it be a certain visiting Irishman?"

"Don't be ridiculous. Craig is leaving soon. I should probably just date more."

"So, I take it last night's date with Hunter didn't go well?"

"It was very nice but…"

"No sparks?"

"Not a one."

"But with Craig…"

"He's coming here this morning to discuss my website."

Grinning, Vivian gave her a little push. "Ah. Now it all makes sense. Tell you what—why don't you go and clean up and I'll try my hand at the scones. I don't have to be at the hospital before ten this morning. I'm no cook as you know, but I think this morning I have a better chance of making scones than you. Go on."

Upset, angry, and irritable, Annie stomped off. At this rate, it was probably a good thing she didn't have any guests—she couldn't even manage something as simple as a scone.

WAY TOO EARLY, Craig parked his car in front of Annie's. He'd said ten and it was half an hour earlier, but he'd been awake since… Well, the truth was, he hadn't really slept. The image of midnight-black sheets and Annie's long legs had kept him awake.

At around five this morning, he'd finally given up and pulled his laptop closer. At least now he had a simple marketing plan for Annie, one that mainly improved on her website so that she could get more traffic.

He'd also phoned Riley this morning to ask if it was possible for her to arrive a few days before the wedding so she could take some new photographs for Annie's website. Riley was thrilled with the idea and eager to help Annie. She'd finished with the works she wanted for her exhibition and she and Dylan would probably arrive in Marietta by Monday. He couldn't wait to see the little guy. At three, Dylan had already managed to wrap his mother and everyone else he came into contact with around his little finger.

The front door opened, Mitch stepped out. He was dressed in a tracksuit, clearly on his way somewhere. Great—at least the brother wouldn't be around this morning.

Cussing beneath his breath, Craig opened the door. The previous time he was here, Mitch had been this nice guy, only growling at Aiden. Now it seemed he'd switched his attention and his wrath on to Craig. Grabbing his laptop, he got out of his car as Mitch approached him.

"O'Sullivan." His eyes fell on the laptop. "You're here to help Annie?"

"I am."

Mitch's frown deepened. "She's burned the scones this morning."

Not quite sure what he was supposed to say, Craig kept his face expressionless. "Does that happen often?"

"Never. So, I want to know if helping Annie with her marketing is the only reason you're here?"

Craig looked away, up at Copper Mountain standing

guard over the town. "I'm leaving after the wedding."

"That's not an answer."

Closing the car door, Craig took a step in the direction of the front door. "That's my answer." Without glancing in Mitch's direction again, he walked farther down the corridor.

Behind him, Mitch cussed, mumbling something about *bloody Irishmen* before he stomped off.

Lifting his hand to ring the bell, Craig frowned. *What's up with the brother? It's not as if I have the hots for Annie …*

He dropped his hand quickly. Of course, he damn well had the hots for Annie. That was the freaking problem. She was beautiful and sweet and honest and he had no business flirting with her and kissing her, let alone propositioning her. Instead, he should encourage her to date that guy she'd been with last night. Annie needed someone for the long haul, not someone like him who knew he wasn't ever getting married.

The proposition he'd had in mind, the one that had nothing to do with any marketing and everything to do with letting Annie kiss him again, should be parked, moved off the table, and out of his mind.

Inhaling deeply, he pressed the bell. Problem was, Annie could never be just another pretty woman he'd flirted with. Truth be told, he was getting worried saying goodbye to her might be way harder than he'd thought.

What he should try and remember was he was here to help her with marketing. Although the plan he'd come up with was a far cry from what he and his team usually did for the big accounts they handled back in Portland, he'd really enjoyed thinking about ways to get a small B and B like Annie's on the map.

The door opened. A grinning Vivian invited him in. "Come on in. Annie will be down shortly."

"I'm a bit early."

Vivian led the way to the kitchen. "Annie was ready but then, strangely enough, there were several incidents with the scones this morning. Her scones are to die for and flop-proof, but, for some or other reason, she's burned the first batch and the second ended up over her feet. So this morning you have the privilege of eating scones I've made. Coffee?"

"Thanks, but I'll wait for Annie."

"I'm here," a soft voice said from behind him.

And there she was—dressed in jeans and a soft lilac top that seemed to bring out her brown eyes. She just about took his breath away. All his resolve to keep his visit strictly business flew out of the window into the glorious morning outside.

"I'm on my way to the hospital." Vivian smiled. "You two have the whole house to yourselves for the rest of the day. Mitch is at school, he's starting early with his cross-country team." With a wave and a smile, she left.

"Coffee? Tea?" Annie asked and without looking at him, she picked up the kettle, filling it with water.

"Whatever you're having," he said, his eyes taking in everything about her. His instinct was telling him to go to Annie, put his arms around her and kiss her, but he valiantly tried to hang on to the last bits of his self-control.

His eyes, though, had a will of their own and took in the way her ponytail bobbed as she moved, the way the jeans hugged every curve of her sexy ass and legs, the slender line of her neck as she turned.

Damn it, he wasn't here to ogle Annie, he was supposed to help her. Forcing himself to look away, he sat down and opened his laptop.

BY THE TIME Annie had made tea, the butterflies had settled to a low buzz in her tummy. She placed the plate of scones Vivian had buttered in the middle of the table before she put Craig's cup in front of him.

Moving to the opposite side of the table, with a pad and pencil in one hand and her cup of tea in the other, she didn't look up. If she could manage not to look him in the eye, she might succeed in not saying something completely inappropriate again.

"So, what other ideas do you have for me?" she asked, keeping her eyes on her tea.

When he didn't react immediately, she quickly looked up.

Blue eyes were intently staring at her. He opened his

mouth, shut it again, and pulled his laptop closer. "Ideas. Right. I have a few. By the way, Riley is finished with what she needed to do for her exhibition. She'll probably arrive Monday or Tuesday to help with new photos. As I've mentioned, you are the brand you want to sell. I've made a list of what backgrounds and poses I think could work. I'll email it to you. Your email?"

Trying to keep her breath even, Annie rattled off her address, opening the pad and picking up the pencil.

Craig cleared his throat. "You had quite an elaborate set-up travelers have to use to make a booking, I've made it simpler. It's difficult enough to compete for traveler attention, there are so many options. Riley's photographs will also go a long way to showcase your uniqueness and the beauty of the surroundings."

Annie was scribbling as fast as she could, but the words she was writing down had no meaning. The mere sound of his voice was driving her crazy. Husky? Exactly as described in the romance novels. She was probably imagining it. Gnashing her teeth, she tried to focus on what he was saying instead of listening to the tone. Swallowing the groan, she tried to focus. *Focus, Annie, focus.*

"You should also partner with online travel agents…" Craig said.

Was it her imagination or was the husky even huskier? She was not going to look up. The pencil hovered over the pad. What had he just said?

"You'd probably have to pay commission fees, but it would be a sure way to put your B and B in front of more travelers," Craig continued.

Annie made a note and waited for his next suggestion, but none came. She was not looking at him again. She waited.

Clearing his throat again, he finally continued. "The sad truth is, of course, it's getting harder to get repeat customers, so what you should focus on is to get referrals and online... Annie, I want to kiss you. That's all I can think about."

Her hand froze, the butterflies in her tummy went crazy, her blood heated, and her heart just about jumped out of body. Had she heard him correctly or had she been dreaming his last sentence? For long minutes, she didn't move.

Finally, she looked up. "You can't say things like that. We both know this can't go anywhere. You're leaving, I have hang-ups and you... I don't even know you, let alone know what hang-ups you may have. This thing between us, is..."

Craig had stood up and was moving toward her. "Have you had wine?"

"It's not even ten o'clock yet!" she cried out. "Of course not."

Slowly, his eyes never leaving her face, he approached her and sat down on the table close to her. "Read any science fiction since I saw you last?"

She glared at him. "It's not helping. All those phrases from all the love stories I've read are still running through my mind!"

"We seem to have a problem then," Craig said. "Number one…" He lifted one finger. "You've dated another man. You even kissed him, but no beading. Number two…" he said, lifting another finger. "You've read a murder mystery and also a science fiction novel, but you're still thinking about the lines from the love stories you've read. And then there's number three…" He held up a third finger. "We are both stone-cold sober and all I can think of is kissing you."

The gasp slipped out before she could stop it. Shoving her chair back, she also got up. She had to try and explain to him why kissing was not a good idea. "Okay, say we kiss and then what?"

He chuckled. "That's not a very difficult one to answer. Then we go to bed. We do have the house to ourselves."

"That's not what I mean!" she cried out. "One time would never be—" Just in time, she swallowed the rest of the words. She couldn't tell him one time with him would never be enough. "Okay, tell me this—do you want to get married?" she asked.

He raised an eyebrow. "Are you proposing?"

She rolled her eyes. "Of course not. I've told you I'm not interested in the wedding-thing again."

"Because of one idiot who was stupid enough to let you go?"

"Well, yes and because…" She threw up her hands. "I'm not interested in climbing the corporate ladder, or office parties, or networking and whatever else professional women do these days. My kitchen is my happy place. I want to stay home and cook for the people I love. I don't care how antifeminist that sounds. I was told men don't like their women like that anymore."

"That is simply not true. Any man would be lucky to have you, Annie Miller. You're smart and beautiful and so sexy you make me ache for you."

She stared at him. He hadn't moved, hadn't touched her, but the whole kitchen was alive with all sorts of strange vibes and electrical currents.

Sighing, she rubbed her temple. "You know my reason for not wanting to get married, what's yours? You also had your heart broken by some woman?"

The one corner of his mouth lifted in a crooked smile. "Nope. I've never been serious enough about anyone to let that happen. Probably had to do with the fact my parents sent me to live with my dad's brother and his wife—Aiden and Riley's parents—when I was ten. My mom and dad are doctors and, I was told, doing important work in underprivileged countries. They joined Doctors Without Borders and have been working overseas since that time. Don't get me wrong, Aunt Cara and Uncle Sean didn't treat me any different to how they did Riley and Aiden. I had a good life with them. Then they both passed away. The three of us were ... are fine, we have each other."

"But they weren't your parents," Annie got out, her heart

breaking for the ten-year-old little boy who had to adjust to a new set of grown-ups only to also lose them. She crossed her arms, making sure she didn't reach out and touch him. "I'm so sorry, you must have been devastated. Is that the reason you don't want to commit? Worried someone else would leave you? Well, let me tell you, Craig O'Sullivan, you're a great guy. You're successful and you're really nice. Any woman would be lucky to have you."

Rubbing his face, he grimaced. "We're all left with scars of some sort from our childhood. Compared to many others, my life has been great. Giving your heart to someone…" He shrugged. "At some point, you'll lose them, it's just a fact. I'm not doing that again."

Annie threw her hands up. "Well, there you have it—the reason we shouldn't kiss. We're both scared of falling in love because we might get hurt."

He picked up one of her hands and absentmindedly played with it. "Up until now, my strategy was to never date just one person at a time."

"Classy." She didn't even try to hide the sarcasm in her voice.

"I mention it up front."

"And that makes it okay? If nobody has told you before, that's a terrible thing to do. Shame on you." Shaking her head, she pulled her hand out of his. "I think we've just established why jumping into bed would be a very bad idea."

He slipped a hand under her hair. "Problem is, I want

you."

"You're leaving."

"I know. I still want you, though." He pulled her closer to him. "You feel what you do to me."

A soft moan slipped over her lips.

He lifted her face up to him. "I have a proposition. If you don't want to do it, it'll probably kill me, but I'll back off and I won't touch you again."

"What kind of proposition?"

"There is something between us."

Rolling her eyes, Annie looked up at him. "The beading and throbbing body parts? I don't know if I'll call that something. That's just lust. It happens…"

"Has it happened with the guy you were with last night?"

"No, but…"

"When I'm near you, I have no control over my body. Neither, it would seem…" Without taking his eyes off of her, he flicked the back of a finger over of those freaking beading nipples of hers. "Have you. I've dated a lot of women, it never happens this way with anyone else."

"A lot?"

"I never date one at a time, remember? My proposition is this—I'm here until the wedding which is in exactly two weeks. Let's spend that time together, dating and whatever else you're comfortable with. Hopefully, this craziness between us will have run its course by the end of that time. We'll be able to agree the beading and the throbbing have been merely lust and move on with our lives. I'll continue helping you with marketing your B and B—which, by the way, I'll do regardless of what you decide."

"And what do we do afterward? My sister is marrying your cousin. We're bound to see one another again. I don't want awkward birthdays and Christmases."

"We'll always be friends, Annie. No matter what you decide to do. And remember, by the time I leave, this—whatever it is between us—would have run its course. Our bodies should be back to behaving."

"Yeah? And what if that doesn't happen?"

"It'll happen, feelings this intense never last."

Swallowing her next words, Annie began pacing. Truth be told, what she felt when she was near Craig was scaring the living daylights out of her. Would spending time together, having sex, really manage to make these feelings evaporate?

She had to think, really think. Being so close to Craig was making it extremely difficult.

Chapter Eight

ANNIE WAS CHEWING her bottom lip as she paced. Every now again, she stopped to look at him. A few times, she opened her mouth, closed it again before resuming the pacing.

Craig watched her intently. What was going on in that mind of hers? He swore he could hear the wheels turning.

When he was about to add something to his argument, she stopped. "Okay, if I agree to your proposition, I have conditions."

Craig swallowed the smile that was threatening to split his face in two. Something was telling him this was so not the time to grin. "Okay, let's hear it."

"One…" she said, lifting a finger in much the same way he'd done earlier. "First, I need time to think about this."

"What do you want to think about? Neither of us wants to get married, right? But we have this thing between us we should explore."

"I still have to think about it."

Rubbing his face, he groaned out loud. "How much time do you need?"

"A week. I don't just jump into bed with every guy I meet. I need to make sure… I need time."

She was right. He knew that. He didn't like it, but she was right. "What is your other condition?"

"We don't tell anyone else about us."

He nodded. "I can agree to that. Less messy that way. What else?"

"I know this may be difficult for you, but my other condition is we don't see other people while we're dating."

Craig pressed his lips together. That was an easy one. He didn't want to be reminded of the date she'd had with what's-his-name. And he couldn't see straight while he was near Annie, let alone think of anyone else. "Agreed."

"Shall we make a date for next Saturday?"

"Do you really need a whole week?" he barked. "That leaves only another week for us to be together."

"Probably not." Tapping a finger against her chin, her tongue chewing her lower lip, she looked out of the window. "But maybe I'll be busy. I may just get all those guests for the spring festival I've been hoping for thanks to you. Okay, what about Wednesday?"

Craig wasn't quite sure what was happening. Annie hadn't rejected his proposition, but he also didn't have permission to take her up the stairs to her room as his whole body was aching to do.

Taking her hand, he pulled her slowly closer. "Okay, Wednesday. In the meantime, I want you to know exactly what happens between us when we kiss…"

Brown eyes darkened. "Not necessary. We've kissed before…"

"Not like this," he whispered against her mouth, giving her ample time to move away if she wanted to. "May I use my hands?" he murmured trailing kisses over her face.

With a groan, her hands slipped around his body. "You m—"

HOT LIPS CAPTURED hers before she could finish the word. His big, warm hands slid restlessly up and down her sides sending her blood to boiling point within milliseconds. Wherever he touched her, she ached until her whole body throbbed in sync with the wild beating of her heart.

This was what she'd wanted, what she'd been dreaming about since she'd seen him the very first time.

He angled his head, deepened the kiss, his tongue curling around hers. Her senses, seeped in the familiar hint of leather and vanilla always surrounding him, blocked out the rest of the world until the only sound she could hear was their ragged breathing. All she could smell was him and all she was aware of was those warm hands restlessly moving over her body.

It was too much, but not nearly enough. Desperate to touch him without any barrier between them, her hands slipped underneath his top and touched his hot, toned flesh. *Oh, my.* Of course, he'd have a six-pack.

With a sigh from deep within her, she explored every one of the tight muscles before her hands glided upward and spread out over his torso. Lifting her head, she grinned. "I'm not the only one beading, it seems."

His eyes were molten sapphire. "I have to see you … touch you." Holding her gaze captive, he opened the top button of her blouse and waited.

Nearly fervent with need, she tried to open the rest, but her hands were shaking too badly and she struggled.

"Let me," he whispered moving her hands aside. His eyes dropped and, one by one, he opened the small buttons. Pulling the two parts to the side, he cussed softly. "Damn, Annie, pink lace … you're killing me." With unsteady hands, he unfastened her bra. "Look at you … so, so beautiful."

Bending down, he closed his mouth over her one breast while his hand fondled the other one. It was all it took for passion to fling her out to sea where wave after wave of pleasure crashed over her, hardly giving her a chance to catch her breath in between. Valiantly, she tried to keep her eyes on him, she wanted to remember this moment, but his onslaught was merciless. Dropping her head backward, she gave herself up to the pure bliss of being loved by someone who knew exactly how to go about doing it.

Nibbling and licking her breasts, Craig was driving her up and up a high mountain until she was just about sobbing out his name.

None of the romances she'd read had been able to describe what she was experiencing in this moment—her last rational thought before she tumbled over the top of the mountain.

HIS BLOOD WAS roaring through his body, urging him on to take what he needed so desperately—Annie. In awe, Craig stared at her. Her skin was hot, her body pliant. If he picked her up now, she wouldn't protest.

But she'd asked for time. She had her conditions. This had to stop before he lost the last vestiges of his self-control and carried her to her bed.

Gulping in air, he kissed Annie's face as she slowly opened her eyes. "Annie, baby..." he muttered, closing her blouse without looking at her gorgeous breasts again. "That was so, so beautiful. You're so beautiful. I want to take you to your bed, but you said you need time..."

For a moment longer, she stared at him, her eyes glazed over with desire, her lips swollen with his kisses.

Frustrated, he dropped a searing kiss on her lips before he turned away. "I'll email you the rest of my ideas. You take your time and read science fiction and keep sober, but I can tell you right now, what has just happened between us is not something you can forget by not thinking about it. Watching you, listening to you while you cry out my name? You have no idea what you do to me." His voice was ragged.

And without looking back at her, he lengthened his strides. He had to get out of here before he did what both of them were desperate to do—make love.

GASPING, ANNIE SAGGED down on the nearest chair. *Oh. My. Goodness.* As long as she lived, she would never forget what had just happened between her and Craig. Her body was on fire and literally aching for more.

Looking down at herself, she groaned and quickly fastened her bra and buttoned up her blouse. She wanted Craig with an intensity that frightened her. She didn't need time to figure that out. But could she just jump into bed with him, make love with him, and blithely walk about days later? She had no intention of going the lets-get-married-route again. Tried that, got hurt, didn't want the T-shirt. However, she had to make sure her heart would survive letting Craig go.

The way he touched her… Oh, my. It was as if he could read her mind, as if he knew exactly how to kiss her, how to touch her, how to lo—With a sigh, she got up and straightened her clothes. She couldn't even think about the L-word. It wasn't on the table—for either one of them.

Her phone rang. Craig? Her heart just about jumped out of her body, but it was an unknown number. *Well, you never know, it could be potential client.*

Rolling her eyes at her own silly thoughts, she answered the call.

Minutes later, she sat down again, dazed. She had guests. Actual guests who'd seen her webpage and wanted to be here for the Spring Arts and Crafts Festival next weekend. Whatever Craig had done to improve her website was obviously working.

She opened her phone. Could she text him after what had just happened? She was the one with the stupid conditions. Well, she had to thank him. Her fingers were flying over the small pad and she pressed send before she could think too much about what she was doing.

I have guests for the spring festival! Thank you.

She stared at the small screen. Her message was delivered, but he hadn't seen it yet. Jumping up, she quickly cleaned the table. Neither she nor Craig had finished their tea or eaten a scone. They had better things to do—they'd been kissing.

Thinking about Craig's lips on hers had her just about salivating. Muttering to herself, she stormed out of the kitchen. Just the mere thought of Craig kissing her, his hands kneading her breasts, had her body humming.

Help. Now she was reciting even more lines from romance novels!

She was going shopping. She had to get out of her house for a while. Besides, she had a good reason—after all the flops this morning she needed to buy flour and eggs.

I T WAS NEARLY lunchtime when Craig jogged up to the front door of his aunt's house. He'd heard his phone bleep earlier, but he'd ignored it. He'd been running.

After he'd returned home from Annie's, the walls of Aunt Janice's house were closing in on him. Maybe a run would clear his head, he'd argued. Something he needed desperately.

Annie's scent was still with him, though, dogging every step of his six-mile run. Damn, the woman was driving him crazy.

Before he could touch the door, it flew open. Aunt Janice stepped out, smiling broadly.

"Well, I've just heard the best news. Annie has guests for the spring festival." She hugged Craig. "Thank you so much. I'm so glad you've agreed to help her. I just knew you would know exactly what to do. Where have you been?"

"I've been for a run. When did you hear that? Have you spoken to Annie?"

"No, Carol Bingley heard Annie telling someone in the pharmacy and then of course she phoned Betty, the police dispatcher, who in turn knew about..."

Craig shook his head. "So, Annie having guests is the talk of the town?"

His aunt grinned. "It's a small town. I'm just so happy for her. Now we just have to find her a nice, steady husband.

I've really hoped she'd like Hunter, but that hasn't worked out." Her eyes widened. "You know, Marcus Baker, the science teacher at our school has been asking about Annie for some time. I'll have to see what Annie says about him. She hasn't dated at all since they've moved here. Understandably, after what has happened to her. All three of those kids are also still hurting because of the way their parents have died. Annie deserves the best, don't you think?"

He nodded. His aunt was right, but he didn't want to think about Annie dating anybody else. "She does, I agree. Please excuse me, Aunt Janice, I need a shower." Turning away, he walked toward his room. His body was still on fire for Annie, but she wanted to think. About what, exactly? They both knew exactly what they wanted and what they wanted was each other. What the hell else was there to think about?

Closing his bedroom door, he checked his phone. His heart kicked against his ribs. Annie had sent a message. But all the message conveyed was to thank him and tell him she had guests for the spring festival.

Peeved, he headed for the bathroom. At least it seemed he could be of some use to Miss Annie.

Minutes later, he had a plan. She hadn't said she didn't want to see him. She just needed time to think about his proposal. Grinning, he got rid of his clothes. He would just have to make sure she didn't forget all about him.

Chapter Nine

B Y SUNDAY NIGHT, Annie was ready to throttle Craig. Not only had he showed up at the pizza parlor while she and her brother had lunch there, he'd also casually strolled into the diner while she was having lunch with Vivian, taking a seat right next to their table and flirting with the waitress. Each time, he'd interrupted them with a big smile before he'd taken his seat at another table.

And lo and behold, here he was again, innocently taking his aunt to dinner. How did he know where she was every time?

Aiden had insisted on taking them all to dinner tonight at the Graff Hotel. Annie had to rest before the rush of guests would arrive next weekend, he'd said. They'd only decided this morning, so how could Craig know she'd be here?

Aiden looked up, saw them, and got up. "Aunt Janice, Craig—how lovely to see you. Join us?"

Aunt Janice smiled broadly. "If you're sure you don't mind?"

"Of course not," Vivian said, getting up as well to hug

98

Janice and Craig.

"Seriously," Mitch mumbled below his breath but he also got up to hug Aunt Janice and shook hands with Craig.

Annie had no choice but to also get up and greet them. She hugged Janice, but only smiled vaguely in Craig's direction. When they'd all taken their seats, Craig was sitting directly opposite her.

By the time the waiter came to whisk their plates away, Annie was so ready to go home. Her neck was strained from trying not to look at Craig, a very difficult task seeing as her eyes seemed to have developed a will of their own and all they wanted was to look at Craig.

Thank goodness for Janice. She'd kept the conversation going. Mitch had been silently glaring in Craig's direction all night and Craig had not once taken his eyes off of Annie.

Again, her eyes turned to Craig. This time, though, he wasn't looking at her as he'd been doing all night. He was looking at his phone, frowning. He looked upset, or was it just her imagination?

Craig got up quickly. "Aunt Janice, are you ready to go?"

Looking slightly baffled, Janice picked up her back. "Of course, my dear."

Dropping way too many bills on the table, Craig walked around the table to help up his aunt.

"Thanks, coz," he said to Aiden and, without looking at Annie again, he and Janice left the restaurant.

Aiden stood standing, staring after them. "Something has

upset him."

"You want to go and talk to him?" Vivian asked.

Aiden sat down. "He'll talk when he's ready. Anyone want anything else?"

Fortunately, nobody wanted anything else to eat or drink and they could leave. Relieved, Annie got up quickly, chewing on her lip. Aiden was right—something Craig had seen on his phone had upset him.

A few minutes later, they were back home. As Mitch closed the door behind them. "I'm off to bed. Thanks for a lovely meal, Aiden."

"You were glaring at poor Craig all night." Vivian chuckled. "I'm amazed you were able to taste anything."

Mitch frowned. "He stares at Annie."

"Of course he does." Vivian laughed, hugging their brother. "She's gorgeous."

Rolling her eyes, Annie opened the front door again. "Good night, everyone. I'm going for a walk."

"I thought we should talk," Mitch said.

"There is nothing to talk about." Quickly, she closed the door behind her and ran down the steps. Her brother meant well, she knew that, but she wasn't ready for any questions tonight.

"THANK YOU FOR tonight." Aunt Janice smiled as they

entered her house. "Something has upset you, though. Want to talk about it?"

"It's nothing really…"

She shook her head. "I know you. What happened?"

"Can we talk tomorrow, please? I need to clear my head. I'm going for a walk."

"Of course, dear. I've really enjoyed having dinner with Annie, Vivian, and Aiden. I love spending time with them. And Annie really is so nice. Red really is her color, don't you think?"

"She looked beautiful," he muttered.

"I must really talk to Annie about Marcus. I'd love to see her settled with a good husband. She deserves all the happiness."

Gnashing his teeth, Craig opened the door. "See you later." His aunt's mouth was opened halfway, but he seriously didn't want to talk about Annie dating other men.

It was cold outside. Putting his hands in the pockets of his jacket, he began walking down the road.

His head was reeling. He was trying to process the message he'd just received but he was struggling. Maybe he should've told his aunt but he hadn't wanted to upset her as well. First, he had to try and make sense of what he'd read.

"Craig?" a soft voice spoke from somewhere close.

Without consciously planning it, his feet had brought him to Annie's house. She was on the sidewalk, illuminated by the streetlight.

"Annie."

She moved closer, chewing her bottom lip. "You followed me yesterday and today."

"I have."

"Why?"

He reached out and touched her face. "You really need to ask me that?"

"I was trying to think about your proposal. Having you close by, has made it difficult."

"Good. Have you finished thinking?"

"You were upset tonight when you left the hotel. Are you okay?" This time, she touched his arm.

Sighing, he pulled her closer. He needed her warmth right now. "What am I going to do about you?" he murmured into her hair.

For long moments, they stood like that. She slowly pulled away. "I firmly believe most things can be solved over a cup of tea. How about it?"

He shook his head. "It's something I have to figure out myself, but thanks. Do you need more time to think?"

"Our last kiss? That was when I've stopped thinking."

Smiling, he slipped a hand under her hair. "And you didn't tell me? I'm very glad to hear that." Pulling her closer, he kissed her.

He'd meant to only tease her lips before he turned back home, but the moment their mouths met, desire reared its head and, with his fingers tangled in her silky hair, he lost himself in her softness.

Somewhere a car started and, out of breath, he lifted his head. Smiling, he combed back her hair, his fingers not quite steady. "Damn, Miss Annie, kissing you is fast becoming addictive."

He had to take a deep breath before he could continue. "Unfortunately, our date will have to be postponed till Tuesday. Riley is arriving tomorrow morning. I thought we could start the photo shoot as soon as she arrives. We should be able to finish Tuesday, though. I can pick you up that evening for our first date? That is, if you're sure you've thought about it long enough?"

One of her brilliant smiles lit up her face. "I'm sure. Thank you."

It was all he could do not to grab her and kiss her again. He took her hand instead. "Let me walk you to the front door. Hopefully, this craziness between us would've run its course by the time I have to leave."

Annie didn't answer. She opened her front door, he gave a step back. If he touched her now, he wouldn't be able to stop.

THE EUPHORIA LASTED until Annie got into bed. Then all the worries and doubts were back. Craig was a hotshot marketing guru from Portland, she was the owner of a struggling B and B in a small town. They had absolutely nothing in common.

Would they have anything else to talk about besides the way their bodies reacted to one another? More importantly, would the obvious spark between them peter out when they spent time together as Craig had predicted? Neither of them was looking for anything permanent, so what would happen when he left and she still wanted him as desperately as she did at this moment?

Looking down at herself, she cupped her breasts. Although, how these could possible react more, she had no idea. They were still happily beading and she'd left Craig about an hour ago.

Dropping her hands to her sides, she stared at the roof. What was the alternative? Tell Craig she didn't want to see him again? That wasn't going to help either. Marietta was a small town, and with the Spring Arts and Crafts Festival next weekend and the wedding right afterward, she was bound to run into Craig.

Her phone bleeped. A message from Craig.

Really like kissing you

And immediately, the beading increased, the butterflies were back, she was just about hyperventilating. Irritated with herself, she rolled her eyes. *Seriously.*

He didn't even want to tell her what was bothering him. She understood that—whatever was going on between them was purely physical. Sighing, she quickly typed a word before she turned off her phone and slid under the covers.

Hopefully, two weeks would be enough time to let the fires the two of them seemed to ignite, slow down and die.

CRAIG STARED AT Annie's message.

Ditto.

A chuckle escaped. Damn, the woman turned him on with a word. Throwing his phone down, he opened his laptop. He wasn't going to sleep; he might as well see what else he could do to help Annie with her marketing.

He'd contacted a colleague on his team who specialized in social-media marketing to ask about the current trends. It had dropped in his inbox sometime today, something he wanted to forward to Annie. Or maybe he should rather talk to her... Chuckling again, he quickly forwarded the email to Annie.

Talking was the last thing on his mind when he was with Annie. Both of them would rather kiss than talk. Not that he had a problem with that. At all. Trouble was, he wasn't sure how he'd ever be able to leave here, knowing he'd never be able to kiss Annie again.

He'd probably see her around when he'd be visiting Aiden and Vivian, but by his next visit, Annie could be with someone. At the moment, she was adamant about not ever getting hitched again, but the right man could change her mind, could persuade her to get married. Annie was meant to have a whole bunch of kids with dogs and a few cats to complete the picture. She was a giver, happiest when she could make others happy.

He leaned back on the bed, stared at the ceiling. Married life. Exactly when he'd taken the decision not ever to get married, he wasn't sure. All he knew was somewhere along the way, he'd realized he wouldn't ever want to do to a kid what his parents had done to him—dropped him off with family without even looking back. He still remembered how long he'd stood on the porch of his uncle's house, waiting for them to wave or look back or something.

And now, according to his father's text he'd received earlier this evening, they were retiring, coming back to Portland. They wanted to see more of him.

Why now? They'd happily lived their lives without ever giving him a second thought. His aunt and uncle were the ones who were there when he'd celebrated a birthday, when he'd fallen and hurt something, who'd never missed a game he'd played in high school, who'd cheered him on from the sides and encouraged him, loved him, and had been there for him.

Until they weren't.

The decision to date more than one person at a time had always worked for him. Everybody knew it was a fun arrangement without any expectations, one that had kept the high walls around his heart intact. Saying goodbye and walking away had never been a problem for him.

Until Annie. They hadn't even been on a date yet, and

he couldn't keep his hands to himself when he was around her.

Saying goodbye to her was not going to be easy.

Chapter Ten

B Y THE TIME Craig, Riley, and Dylan arrived at her B and B on Monday, Annie was in a state. She'd even gone so far as to phone one of the real estate businesses in town to ask their valuation team to have a look at her house.

The email Craig had forwarded yesterday, had her just about hyperventilating when she'd read the suggestions. There was no way she could do any of this. Selling the place sounded infinitely easier than trying all the stuff the email listed.

Know your followers, he'd said. But how could she know who her followers were if she didn't have any? Pick a platform, was another idea but she'd never been on any social media, so she had no idea what to pick. Sharing her every waking moment with perfect strangers had never sounded like any fun to her. Apparently, there was also a "seven and one" rule when it came to advertising her B and B. She couldn't simply market her services over and over, she had to write posts that were relevant and beneficial and, oh, also interesting to her customers before she could post one advertisement.

What would she write about? The only thing consuming her thoughts at the moment was Craig O'Sullivan. Probably not a topic to discuss on social media.

Annie hugged Riley. "I'm so glad you're here, although I have to warn you, this may all be in vain. I'm thinking of selling the place." Crouching down, she smiled at Riley's little boy who was hiding behind his mother's legs. "Hi, Dylan, I'm so glad to meet you." She held out her hand.

Shyly, the little boy took her hand, but disappeared behind his mom's legs again.

"Why do you want to sell?" Craig asked as she stood up. "Haven't you recently spent a lot of money converting it to exactly what you want?"

"Yes, but the last email you've forwarded just about broke my spirit." She opened the door wider. "Sorry, come on in. I've made croissants."

They walked through to the kitchen where Vivian was with her mug of coffee.

"Riley!" She smiled and hugged her soon to be sister-in-law. "I'm on my way to the hospital, but I hope we can catch up tonight?" She bent down to talk to Dylan.

"Yes, please, Riley," said Annie. "Come for dinner and do bring Janice along, she hasn't visited in a while."

"Sounds great," Riley said. "How have you been?" she asked Vivian and the two of them with Dylan tagging along, moved to the other side of the kitchen.

"What about me?" Craig asked, touching Annie's hand.

"What do you mean?" Annie asked as Craig laced his fingers with hers.

"Am I also invited to dinner?"

"Of course, you are. But, Craig, I'm serious. I don't know if I can do this marketing thing. Maybe I have to make peace with the fact that I don't have what it takes to run a B and B. I like talking to people face-to-face. I want to cook for them, make them feel welcome. But doing all that stuff mentioned in the email you've forwarded…" She groaned. "I'm not good at that!"

"Annie, baby, breathe." Pulling out a chair, he gently pushed her down. "Inhale, exhale, come on…" he murmured, sitting down on another chair close to her.

Looking up at him, she concentrated on her breathing for a few minutes.

"There we go," he crooned, tucking her hair behind her ear. "At least you have your color back again. For a minute there, I was worried you'll keel over."

"I can't do this, Craig," she cried out softly.

"Of course, you can," he said gently, taking her hand again and cupping her face with his other hand. "You're so strong, I'm in awe of you. We'll take it one step at a time. Riley is here, we'll do the photos today and tomorrow. As soon as they are up on your website, we can try one or two more things. You don't have to do it all. That email I've forwarded are suggestions, that's all. The few tweaks we've made to your website have already generated interest."

"What you've done are more than mere *tweaks*. I'm hopeless with that stuff."

"For the next two weeks, I'm here and I'll help. Can I now please get an Annie-smile?"

Smiling tremulously, she looked at him.

His eyes darkened. "Damn, I love your smile. Only now I want to kiss you," he whispered.

"What the hell is going on here?" Mitch's voice thundered close by.

Grimacing, Craig sat back in his chair.

Annie tried to pull her hand out of Craig's, but he wouldn't let go.

"Oh, yes, the angry brother." Riley chuckled as she and Vivian approached the table. "I've forgotten all about him. Haven't eaten yet? Or is this your normal morning routine?"

Mitch's eyes narrowed. "Riley. Didn't know you were here."

"Annie," asked Riley, her eyes still on Mitch, "do you want Mitch in any of the photos?"

"I don't know," Annie said. "Mitch?"

"It's Annie's house," Mitch growled. "I'm just here temporarily."

"Good," said Riley drily. "I don't know if being angry is your normal expression, it's the only one I've seen so far, but it's not a look beneficial to generate traffic to Annie's website or her B and B."

For a moment, Annie was worried Mitch was going to

explode.

"Why is the man yelling, Mommy?" Dylan whispered loud enough for all to hear.

Mitch inhaled slowly and, with a glare in Craig's direction, he walked toward Dylan. Crouching down in front of the little boy, he held out his hand. "I'm sorry I yelled. Your uncle Craig is holding my sister's hand and I want to know why."

Dylan peered around Mitch to look at them. "Have you asked him?"

Everyone laughed and Mitch stood up. "Good idea. Why are you holding my sister's hand, O'Sullivan?"

"Because I like it," Craig said.

"If you mess with her…" he began but at that moment, Aiden strolled in.

"Why is Mitch bellowing again?" Aiden asked no one in particular.

"Your damn cousin," Mitch got out.

"Language," Riley said mildly.

Pulling her hand from Craig's, Annie jumped up. "Seriously, Mitch. Relax. Craig is helping me with my website." Looking at Craig, she inhaled. She hadn't wanted to have to explain anything to anyone, but Mitch's behavior is driving her nuts. "Craig's here for another two weeks, during which time he'll be helping me. We've also decided to spend time together so you'll have to get used to Craig being around."

Mitch began to splutter, Vivian and Aiden's eyes widened, and Riley laughed as she clapped her hands.

Annie ignored them all. "Neither one of us is interested in anything more than having fun, though. So Mitch, please relax and stop looking daggers at Craig. Riley, I'm ready if you want to start. But please—we could always do later today if you need to rest?"

Opening her camera bag, Riley grinned. "I'm fine."

The doorbell rang.

Riley put up her hand. "That would be the makeup artist and hairdresser. I took the liberty of contacting the local florist, Risa Davison to ask whom she'd recommend. She remembered Aiden—the guy who had to buy flowers for two women to apologize." She chuckled. "Annie, I hope you don't mind? You're, of course, beautiful just as you are but for photographs you'll need more makeup."

"Of course not." Flustered, Annie opened a cupboard and got out some toys that had belonged to her and Mitch and Vivian as well as new ones she'd bought for the children of all those hordes of visitors she was going to have.

As usual, she'd combed her hair and put on lipstick this morning. During the day she didn't bother with makeup, really, her kitchen didn't mind. However, Riley obviously didn't think she was B and B advertising material.

"I'm out of here," Mitch mumbled.

"So am I." Vivian smiled as she grabbed Aiden's hand. "Walk with me?"

Someone touched Annie's shoulder. Craig. She didn't

have to turn around to know it was him. Every delicious chill sliding down her spine was telling her.

"Riley is a professional. Getting makeup artists and hairdressers is part of what she does, it doesn't mean anything else."

"No matter what they do with their magic brushes, I'm still me. Plain Annie. I shouldn't be in any of the photographs. Why don't you—"

Craig bent down and kissed her. "You're beautiful, Annie Miller, just the way you are." Winking, he smiled. "So now you've told everyone we'll be spending time together. I thought one of your conditions was not to tell anyone about us."

Blushing again, Annie groaned. "Well, you were holding my hand and wouldn't let go. I hadn't planned on making an announcement. It's just… Mitch makes me so mad. I love him to bits, but he can take the protecting brother thing a tad too far. Please don't feel you have to—" she began but he caught her close.

"You know exactly what you do to me. I can't wait to spend more time with you."

"You're not worried the whole thing may be too messy now that everyone knows about us?"

Smiling, he kissed her forehead. "Life is messy, baby, I've realized. Go on, enjoy the photo shoot. Oh, and Riley will also help you set up an account on social media."

Annie groaned out loud. "Do I have to?"

"You don't have to do all. Pick one. I'd go for one where pictures are important."

"Okay, I'll talk to Riley."

"You'll be great. I'll pop in later."

"Won't you be here?" she asked nearly panicking.

Smiling, Craig trailed a hand down her face. "Riley knows what she wants to do. I'll only interfere. You've got this."

With a last soft kiss, he left the kitchen just as Riley entered with two women.

"Annie, meet Marlene and Sienna Murphy."

Annie smiled. "Hello and welcome. Two sisters?"

Looking at the two women, Riley grinned. "Told you. No, Marlene is Sienna's mom."

"Wow, you look so young!" Annie exclaimed. "Well, as you can see…" she said, gesturing to her face, "you have your work cut out for you."

Sienna shook her head as she approached Annie. "I don't know what idiot led you to believe that, but you're gorgeous. Mom, look at these cheekbones! You are one of those natural beautiful women who doesn't really need makeup. We'll just enhance what is already there. Mom does the hair, I'll do the makeup."

As the two women carried on discussing what they wanted to do, Riley took out a coloring book for Dylan.

Annie motioned the little boy closer. "I also have something for you." She smiled, pointing toward the toys. She got her first tentative smile from the little guy. Uncertainly, he came closer.

Annie took out some of Mitch's old cars and placed them on the carpet. "Come on, let's race." She smiled. Within seconds, the little boy was on his knees next to her. Behind them, she heard Riley's camera clicking away. Probably photos of the kitchen.

"Craig has very definite ideas of what he thinks will work, but if you have any suggestions, please tell me," Riley said. "He mentioned a hammock?"

Blushing, Annie stood up, keeping her face averted. That was where all her problems had started. If it hadn't been for the hammock and romance books, there wouldn't have been any freaking beading. "It's outside. Let's try Craig's suggestions and see. Hopefully that will be enough."

Chapter Eleven

F EELING STRANGELY AT a loss, Craig drove to Main
Street. It wasn't as if he didn't have work, a number of
emails were waiting for his attention. There was a restlessness
inside of him, though, that was making it difficult to focus
on work. A first. He'd never before experienced this. Up
until now, his work life had been all consuming. Until...

With a sigh, he stared at the quaint storefronts of the
shops lining the street.

His thoughts turned to the last account his team had
won. He was still uneasy about the whole thing. For the first
time since he'd started working, he was questioning the way
they did business. It was one thing winning an account but
to find out the other side had to close down? He couldn't
simply brush the thought aside like his colleagues seemed to
be able to do.

To be honest, he'd enjoyed the last few days helping Annie to get more clicks on her website. It wasn't merely a job;
he was trying to help the person behind the business. He was
helping someone, not tearing anything or anyone down. It
had made all the difference.

Main Street was busy. When he'd been here in February, there hadn't been much time to explore, but he'd often thought of the small town over the last couple of months. With classic Western storefronts, mountains surrounding it, Marietta was a truly beautiful town.

He remembered Aunt Janice talking about the history of the town. When copper was found in the nearby Butte, miners and prospectors, all eager to get rich, flooded Marietta. Turned out, though, the copper in Copper Mountain was more like fool's gold and the mining ceased within ten years. The few folks who had stayed behind after most had left, as well as immigrants from Europe, started putting down roots, raising cattle and working the land and today Marietta was a thriving community.

Annie should put something about this on her website. Quickly, he got out his phone and left her a voice note.

He hadn't really seen much of the town so far. During his previous visits, he'd mostly been around the family and Annie. And well, this time round, things hadn't really changed. Somehow he was still always around Annie.

A sign saying JAVA CAFÉ caught his eye. Coffee was always a good idea. As he got out of the car, he noticed the pharmacy on the opposite corner. Before he had his coffee, he should pop in there. If he were to spend time with Annie, as she'd told everyone this morning, they'd probably end up in bed at some point. He had to be prepared. Though how it would be possible was another question—there were always family around.

In the pharmacy, he quickly found what he wanted and joined the short line waiting to pay. It went slowly. The woman behind the till seemed to know everyone and didn't finish a sale until she'd gathered a lot of info from her customer. Nobody seemed in a hurry, so he tried to relax.

From behind him came a low chuckle. He turned around. A pretty woman with dark curly hair and laughing brown eyes was eyeing the three packages in his hand.

"Sorry," she said. "You're new in town, aren't you?"

"Visiting."

"Any relation to Aiden and Riley O'Sullivan?" Motioning toward his hair, she grinned. "Quite distinctive. I'm Risa Davison. I own the flower shop in town. For in case you also need to apologize to someone, like your cousin did."

"Um ... thanks, I..."

"Next!" the woman behind the till called.

Relieved, Craig stepped forward. He wasn't quite sure how to respond to the woman behind him. Putting the package on the counter, he reached for his wallet. Probably good to know who owned the flower shop, though. As she'd said, for in case.

The woman behind the counter raised her eyebrows. "You want all three boxes of condoms?" She seemed to have only one volume and that was very loud.

"Yes, please," Craig said, his thoughts already back to the flower shop. What kind of flowers did Annie like? He still knew so little about her. She was beautiful and kind and cooked like an angel. He didn't know what flowers she liked, though, or what her favorite song was or…

"Thank you," said the woman and he grabbed the packet, heading for the door.

What he did know was that Annie Miller did something to him he didn't quite understand. Trying to figure out why was driving him nuts. She was beautiful, but he knew many pretty women. She was sexy, but so were many other women. There was just something about Annie that kept her in his thoughts. It was unexpected. Also disturbing, if he were honest.

Java Café was busy. He took a seat at a table near the back. A paper laid on it, upside down. *Bozeman Daily Chronicle*. Picking up the paper, he grinned. Who still read an actual paper? He placed his order for coffee before he opened it.

The main news article was about a big federal funding for a project to thin trees and treat noxious weeds on public and private land around the Gallatin Valley.

His coffee arrived. As he closed the paper, his eye fell on the property section—office spaces for sale. As he picked up the paper again, someone cleared his throat close by. Craig turned his head.

A big man was standing next to his table. "You thinking of staying here?" the man asked. "You should stop at the real estate office down the street, corner of Main and First."

"Thanks, but I'm just reading the paper," Craig said.

"Hear you're helping Annie Miller with marketing. If you've got time, I'd like to talk to you." Not waiting for Craig to answer, the man pulled out a chair.

IT WAS NEARLY four o'clock before Riley was happy. Dylan was just waking up from a nap he'd had on the couch. Annie was so tired, she dropped down on the first chair. She'd smiled and posed for hours.

During the time her hair and makeup had been done, Riley had also found time to set up an account for her on Instagram. Riley, Marlene, and Sienna all thought that was the best platform for the B and B. It looked quite easy, but whether she'd have something to post every day, was another matter.

"Wow, that was intense," she got out.

Looking still as radiant and unflappable as she had early this morning, Riley put her camera down. "You were great. I think Craig will be so happy. Are you sure about tonight? You're not too tired?"

Smiling, Annie jumped up. "Of course not. Cooking energizes me, it makes me happy."

Before she'd finished speaking, Riley had picked up her camera again and was merrily clicking away. "You literally light up when you talk about cooking." Riley smiled. "Sorry,

I had to take those."

"I love it, always have."

"That's the kind of thing you'd share on Insta. You now have an account. All you need to do is post pictures or videos every day. Consistency is important when advertising on social media."

"Videos? Seriously? I have no idea where to start."

Riley laughed. "I'll show you, don't worry. People like real, in-the-moment glimpses of your life and that's why short videos make a difference when selling your brand on social media."

"Really? My life is pretty boring, but, okay, I'll try. And please send me your bill, I've taken up so much of your time…"

Riley picked up her son. "Don't be silly. We're family. Besides, I've—"

Before she could finish her sentence, Mitch stormed into the kitchen. "Where the hell is O'Sullivan?"

"The man is yelling again, Mommy," Dylan said pointing at Mitch.

Clearly highly amused, Riley put up her hand. "Indeed, he is, sweetie. Apparently, his mood has not improved during the day."

Mitch glared at her. "Not you. I'm looking for your cousin—where is he?"

He was still hopping mad, but at least his voice had dropped a few octaves.

"You bellowed?" Craig asked as he also entered the kitchen.

Mitch rounded on him. "Do you have any idea what you've done? Buying condoms from Carol Bingley of all people in the middle of the morning for all to see and hear— what the hell were you thinking?" Mitch's voice had raised several decibels again.

"What's con-condoms, Mommy?" Dylan asked with big eyes.

Chuckling, Riley quickly whispered something in Dylan's ear.

Annie's eyes found Craig's. The butterflies went crazy and there were definitely some beading happening. Oh. My. He'd bought condoms.

Craig winked at her before he faced Mitch. "You really want to get into that now?"

Mitch turned red.

Stepping forward, Annie laid a hand on her brother's arm. "Mitch, sweetie, what is wrong with you? I'm not sure what's gotten into him," she said to Riley and Craig. "My brother is usually a teddy bear."

"Really?" Riley chuckled. "Has someone eaten his porridge then?"

Inhaling sharply, his eyes wide, Dylan looked at his mother. "Goldilocks?" he whispered loud enough for all to hear.

Craig's lips twitched. Mitch glared at him.

"The whole town," Mitch told Annie, "knows what he's bought. Not one, not two—but three freaking boxes. There's a wager when and where he's going to use them."

"My goodness, people are clearly very bored around here," Riley said before she smiled at her cousin. "I think it went well this morning, Craig. I'm very happy with what we've done. Annie is a natural. I'll see you in the car," she said to Craig, struggling with Dylan and her camera.

Mitch held out his hands to Dylan. "Let me help you."

"I'm fine," Riley said.

"No, you're not," Mitch replied as the little boy went to Mitch without hesitation.

Annie smiled. Mitch loved kids and had a way with them. Apparently, Dylan instinctively knew that.

"Are you going to yell again?" Dylan asked.

"Finished for the day," Mitch said gravelly.

Dylan smiled. "I'm glad. I don't like yelling."

Riley turned to leave the kitchen. "That would be a nice change." Mitch, with Dylan in his arms, followed her outside.

"You've bought condoms?" Annie whispered as soon as they were out of ear shot.

Grinning, Craig pulled her closer. "I have. Sorry, I hadn't realized the very talkative woman behind the till was the Carol Bingley I've been hearing about since Aiden arrived in Marietta."

"Everybody in town will know what we're going to do."

"Then we can't disappoint them, can we?" He chuckled before he kissed her quickly. Frowning, he looked down at her. "Are you okay with that? I'm sorry, I honestly didn't know buying condoms was a thing."

Annie shrugged. It was going to be a while before the rumors died down. If people knew she was sleeping with Craig, so be it. Craig was leaving soon; he wouldn't be around to experience the gossiping mill at work. "It's a very small town. People talk."

"I want to kiss you, but Riley and Dylan are waiting."

"Of course. I'll walk you out."

"I had quite an interesting morning," Craig said as they walked toward the front door.

"What happened?"

"After my pharmacy stop, I had coffee in Java Café. Turns out quite a few folks around town are looking for help with marketing."

Grinning, Annie rolled her eyes. "They do know you're a hotshot from Portland, working with accounts from big corporations?"

"Marketing is marketing."

"That's simply not true and you know it. Thanks for asking Riley to help, but I really do want to pay her for her time. She's brilliant."

"That she is. She's happy to help—let her?" Taking her hand, they walked down the steps toward his car.

Mitch was putting Dylan in his chair in the back while a

frowning Riley was watching his every move.

Craig dropped a quick kiss on Annie's lips. His mouth was hot, urgent, and left her breathless. His eyes had darkened. "See you tonight."

CRAIG WAS AWARE of Riley's eyes on him all the way back to Aunt Janice's house.

As he parked the car, she touched his arm. "You falling for Annie?"

"We're having a bit of fun, that's all. Like me, she's not interested in anything more permanent." Quickly, he got out of the car to help her with Dylan.

Riley was already opening the door at Dylan's side. "I've never seen you like this with anyone else."

"I'm leaving."

Craig picked up Dylan and headed for the front door. Talking about his feelings was so not what he was comfortable with.

Riley wasn't finished with him yet. "So, how is this going to work? After the wedding you'll simply go back to Portland? Will you start dating two women at a time again?"

Shrugging, he opened the front door. "Probably."

"And what about Annie?"

Sighing, he put Dylan down. "Look, I don't know. All I know is I want to be with her while I'm here. That's it."

"Who's the *her* you want to be with?" Aunt Janice asked as she approached them from the direction of the kitchen.

"He likes Annie." Riley grinned. "But he's still figuring out how much. Let me know if you're struggling, I'll tell you exactly what's going on. Annie has announced to all this morning they'll be spending time together."

Aunt Janice smiled uncertainly. "Annie? I hope you're not going to break her heart? She's still recovering from having lost her parents."

"Do you know what happened?" Riley asked his aunt. "I've heard the Millers parents' deaths were very tragic, but I don't know what happened."

Aunt Janice sighed. "Such a sad story. Their mom was a social worker. Whenever he could, their dad would accompany her when she visited the seedier parts of Sacramento. On one such occasion they were the victims of a drive-by shooting."

"Oh, no!" Riley called out, her eyes filling with tears. "How absolutely dreadful. Is that why they'd moved here?"

His aunt nodded. "One of the reasons. Remember Vivian's bad experience with the boss she had at the hospital she was working at in Sacramento. Mitch was in finance, apparently, but he's always wanted to write a novel. He was the one who suggested they move across state lines. Annie remembered the happy holiday they had visiting Yellowstone National Park and the beautiful town they'd seen on their way and well, here they are." She turned to Craig again. "Be gentle with Annie. She's not like the women you normally date and discard."

Craig gave his aunt a hug. "We're both in this with eyes wide open. She doesn't want to get married and neither do I. For the next two weeks we're spending time together. That's it."

"That's a pity. I had high hopes for her and Marcus Baker." She smiled. "But I'll tell Marcus to wait until you've left."

Irritated, Craig turned to go to his room, but Aunt Janice touched his arm. "We have to talk."

His aunt's eyes were troubled. "Everything okay?" he asked.

She pulled him into the living room. "Your dad has just called me. He says he's sent you a message to tell you they're back in Portland. For good. That's why you've been upset."

Rubbing his face, Craig sighed. "Yeah. I got their message yesterday. I'm not sure why they want to see me, though?"

"They… um, they'll be arriving in Marietta tomorrow."

Taken aback, Craig stared at his aunt. He wasn't quite sure how to react. "Will they be staying with you?"

"No, I've suggested Bramble House."

His mind in a turmoil, Craig turned away. "Thanks for letting me know. Annie is expecting us around seven this evening. We can take my car."

Why would his parents want to see him now? The few

holidays he'd spent with them had been few and far between. During those weeks, they'd be busy, not quite sure what to do with him. Later, he'd found excuses not to go. They'd sent presents but because they didn't know him, they had no idea what he'd liked and sometimes it was clear they hadn't even been sure how old he was.

Annie. He wanted to go to her. Right now. She'd know something was wrong. She'd know what to say.

Closing his bedroom door behind him, he walked toward the windows looking out over Copper Mountain.

He'd worked hard to keep his work and private life separate. Not that there had ever been much of a private life. Work had always been his sanctuary. Usually, he was the calm and centered one in the room. He hated chaos and always planned everything to the last detail.

That had all changed after the last big account they'd won.

Coming here, visiting Aunt Janice, had probably been the most spontaneous thing he'd ever done. Since then, being spontaneous came easily. Like kissing Annie.

His phone rang. Without checking his phone, he answered.

His thoughts racing, he dropped his phone a few minutes later. Another resident of the small town of Marietta seemed to need his services.

Interesting.

Someone knocked on his door. "It's Riley. I have some

pictures I want you to look at."

"Come on in," he called.

Riley entered with Dylan right behind her.

"You mind?" Riley asked, pointing at her son.

Bending down, he picked up the little boy. "Of course not. I've missed you guys."

Dylan laid his head against Craig's shoulder. Swallowing the strange lump in his throat, Craig hugged the small body.

Smiling, Riley opened her laptop. "You're so good with him. You should marry and get a few of those yourself."

"Don't be ridiculous. I'm not dad material—wouldn't know what to do with a kid. Let me see?"

"You'd better sit down, there are quite a few."

Settling Dylan on his lap, he took the laptop from Riley. Annie smiled up at him from the computer screen. *Damn, she's beautiful.*

Riley's hand moved in front of him and she swiped over the screen.

"Look at her—she literally lights up when she talks about food. I see that same look on her face when you come into a room," Riley added, her voice softer.

Craig scrolled through the pictures—all photos of Annie in different poses. In one, she was playing with Dylan, another she was lying on the hammock, there she was tasting food, her lips around a spoon.

His body tightened. Damn, he had it bad—whatever "it" was.

Riley took her laptop from him. "I've sent you the ones I like best. I've also taken some photos of Copper Mountain and tomorrow I thought I'd take a stroll down Main Street. Such a quaint town."

"Thanks, Riley." Kissing Dylan's head, he slid the little boy to the floor. "Did you have time to help her with social media?"

"I've set up an Insta account for her and have posted two of the pictures I've taken this morning. It's a whole new world to her."

"Thanks for your help."

Riley took Dylan's hand. "Of course. I like Annie. She brings out the best in you. And just so you know—you're amazing with kids, you always have been. Since Dylan's birth, you were there for me and for him. You moved in with me, helped me through those first three months."

"Anybody would've done the same."

"No, they wouldn't, but you did. You'll be a great dad, if you let go of all the doubts you have about yourself. You're a great human being, Craig O'Sullivan. My life and Dylan's are richer because you're in it." With a wave of her hand, she left, closing the door softly behind her.

Craig sat staring at the door. Kids. Wife. A house in the suburbs. A dog. He'd never allowed himself to go there, to even contemplate the possibility of being a husband, a father. He wouldn't know how to do it, he'd always told himself. His own parents hadn't wanted him around. There had to be something wrong with him or he had done something...

The thought popped into his head out of nowhere. It hadn't been something he'd ever consciously thought, but there it was, hidden in his subconscious, ready to fill his thoughts whenever his parents were mentioned.

Restless, he got up and walked toward the window again. Riley's beautiful photo of Annie playing with Dylan ran through his mind. She'd be a wonderful mother. A little boy with his momma's big, brown eyes...

His phone bleeped. A message from his father. Grimacing, he opened the message. He had no idea what to say to them.

Chapter Twelve

"I AM SO, so late," Annie murmured as she finally stormed back into the kitchen.

The food was finished, the table laid, but she had trouble deciding what to wear. Most of her wardrobe was still lying on her bed. She'd finally settled for a pair of blush-pink soft palazzo pants with a white halter top, items she'd bought the last time she'd been to Bozeman with Vivian. The pair of boho hoop earrings with different colored stones all around the hoop, a present from Vivian last Christmas, added a bit of a wow-factor to any outfit.

It wasn't quite spring yet, but the house was nice and warm, she wouldn't be cold.

She had just put the flowers on the table when the front doorbell rang.

"Are we expecting company?" Mitch asked from the kitchen. The kitchen, dining and living room were one big open space and they usually ate in the kitchen, but tonight she'd laid the big dining room table.

"The O'Sullivans are coming for dinner. My way of thanking Craig and Riley for what they've done. Do you mind getting the door? And Mitch?"

"Yeah, yeah, I won't yell," he grumbled as he left the kitchen.

Sighing, Annie added the finishing touches before she stepped away from the table. She'd always enjoyed making things pretty and she absolutely loved making a table inviting for her guests. Whether she was having people or only cooking for her family, she delighted in the whole ritual of putting down knives and forks, deciding on the plates, the flowers and candles. Always, always candles. Like her mom used to have.

"Oh, Annie—this looks so beautiful!" Janice called out as she came closer, Dylan's hand in hers. "Riley—come and have a look."

Annie crouched down. "Hi Dylan."

Smiling, the little boy threw his arms around her neck. "I like you, Annie."

Laughing, she hugged him. "I like you too."

As she got up, Riley was walking toward them, camera in hand. "Hope you don't mind, I also wanted to capture this evening." Lifting her camera, she began clicking away. "Aunt Janice you're right—she does this beautifully."

Annie smiled and nodded, but her eyes were searching for Craig. And there he was, entering the kitchen with his cousin Aiden.

Their eyes met. Something was wrong. There was a tightness around his mouth she hadn't seen before. Excusing herself from Riley and Janice, she walked toward him.

"Everything okay?" she asked when she reached him, touching his arm.

Pulling her closer, he hugged her, pressing his mouth against her naked shoulder. "Missed you. You look incredible. How the hell am I supposed to keep my hands to myself?" He touched her earrings. "I love these."

Smiling, she searched his face. He wasn't going to tell her what was bothering him. "Missed you, too."

"Okay, you two," Mitch grumbled. "How about we eat first?"

"Is Vivian back from the hospital?" Annie asked Aiden.

"She should be here any minute now," Aiden said just as the front door opened. Smiling, Aiden turned away quickly. "And there she is."

STARING AFTER HIS cousin who was just about running to see his soon-to-be wife, Craig put an arm around Annie. Aiden was clearly besotted with his fiancé and she with him. They made being together look so easy.

"Craig?" Annie asked.

He wanted to talk to her, to tell her what was bothering him, but he wasn't staying around—what was the point? They were supposed to have a little fun, not share painful memories with one another.

Instead, he stroked the satin softness of her shoulders. "This is driving me crazy."

Catching her breath, she grabbed his wandering hand, pulling him closer to where the rest were standing around the dining room table. "Behave. I have people to feed. Come on, I need a glass of wine."

"Lovely flowers," he said, pointing toward the red lilies on the table. "Your favorite?"

Smiling, she shook her head. "I love all flowers, but there is just something about a bunch of red roses, you know? I can't wait for summer so I can fill the house with them. These are amaryllis."

"I'm learning more about you every day," he said softly. "Red roses?"

"Love them," she smiled.

Mitch had already opened a bottle and was handing out glasses to Aunt Janice and Riley.

"Have you told Annie your parents will be here tomorrow?" Riley asked.

Craig swallowed his groan. With a family like his, keeping personal stuff personal was just about impossible. He should've known either his cousin or his aunt would say something.

ANNIE DROPPED HIS hand. "It's fine. I'm sure he doesn't

want to share all his personal stuff with us. I'm going to get the food... Hi, Viv." She smiled as Aiden and Vivian reached them. "Will you make sure everyone has a seat? I'm getting the food."

Gnashing his teeth, Craig quickly followed her. He was fairly positive Riley knew he hadn't planned on telling Annie about his parents arriving tomorrow. That was why she'd mentioned it. And really, it wasn't that big a deal, he probably would've said something eventually. Now it was a thing.

He caught Annie's arm in the kitchen. "Annie, baby, it's not that I wasn't going to tell you …"

Smiling at some spot way above his head, Annie shook her head. "Don't worry about it. We kiss and make out, no personal details needed. Will you please take this through to the table for me?"

"What can I do?" Mitch asked as he approached them.

Pressing his lips together, Craig took the tray with casseroles Annie had given him to the table. Damn it to hell—there was never a moment without hordes of family surrounding them.

BY THE TIME Annie had finally finished cleaning the kitchen, it was after eleven. Thousands of thoughts were racing through her head; there was no way she was going to fall asleep.

Without knowing why, she was upset and wanted to cry. She and Craig had a deal, if she could call it that. They'd have fun for a few days. That was it. There was no reason to be upset because he hadn't told her about his parents visiting Marietta. It wasn't as if they were planning on sharing their life together.

Switching off the lights, she headed toward her room. At the front door, she stopped. A walk would maybe clear her head. Grabbing a jacket from the cupboard next to the door, she opened it and slipped outside. Vivian, Aiden, and Mitch had helped with the cleaning up, but she'd sent them away at some point.

She'd hoped having silence around her would help to calm her mind, but there were serious size beetles jumping around in there.

The air was crisp and cold and huddling in her jacket, she inhaled deeply. As she stepped down the last stairs, a lone figure approached her. Even before she could see his face clearly, her body recognized Craig. And reacted. *Oh, my goodness.*

"We should stop meeting like this." She smiled.

"You've been quiet tonight."

"It's not as if I'm ever the belle of the ball."

He'd reached her and took her hand. "Yeah, but I know you. I'm sorry for not telling you…"

"It's totally fine…"

"No, it's not. Can we talk?"

"Of course. Come on in. The others have gone to their rooms. What about a nightcap?"

"Nothing for me, thanks."

She took him to her office and closed the door behind them. Hopefully, Mitch wouldn't feel he had to barge in here to save her honor or something.

Instead of sitting down next to her on the couch, Craig began pacing. "There isn't really that much to tell. The bottom line is, I don't have any sort of relationship with my parents. I've told you I've lived with my dad's brother, Uncle Sean and his wife Cara, Aiden and Riley's parents since I was ten. My parents did visit, they'd come back for short periods during which time I'd stay with them, but…"

Annie didn't take her eyes off of Craig as he talked. Stunned, she listened as he tried to rationalize why his parents had left him with family, but damn it, he'd been ten—there was no rationalizing leaving your ten-year-old boy for months at a time with someone else even if they were family.

"And now they're back for good." Craig stopped. "They want to see me. They're arriving in Marietta tomorrow. My father sent another message. They want to see me tomorrow. And I … I don't know if I have anything to say to them."

"Have you ever told them how you feel about having been left behind?"

"It's not … I don't …" Rubbing his face, he dropped down next to her on the couch. "Talking about feelings isn't something I do."

"Then maybe it's time. It's probably also time to realize the fact that you were left behind wasn't because of anything you'd done."

Surprised, he looked at her. "I've only just realized that subconsciously I've always thought that and you put your finger right on it in moments. I was mostly angry and hurt."

Annie took his hand. "I'm no psychologist, but any child who has been in your position would probably think he must have done something very wrong. Why else would his parents just simply leave him? On top of that, you're probably also feeling guilty because you're angry. Your parents are saving lives, doing good, after all."

For long minutes, he sat staring in front of him. "They hadn't wanted me around. That was the one thing that kept going around in my mind. It still does, if I'm honest. But I've never acknowledged, never put into words the fact that I also thought their leaving me behind was my fault. And that I am feeling guilty about being angry." Turning to her, he cupped her face. "You're a wise woman, Annie Miller. I'm lucky to know you. May I now please kiss you? All the talk about feelings is not my thing, but I do know what I feel when I'm with you."

"You ma—" She didn't get to finish the word.

Craig's lips were hot and urgent and desperate and within minutes she was burning up, just about climbing on to his lap.

Gasping, he lifted his head, his eyes nearly black with desire. "I want to see you." Impatiently, he tugged at the bow at the back of her neck. "How the hell do I open this thing?"

Breathlessly, she laughed. "Untie it."

Cussing under his breath, he tried.

"Let me?" She smiled and with her eyes never leaving his face, she loosened the bow and let it drop.

His eyes held hers for a moment longer before he looked down. Inhaling deeply, he cupped her breasts with both hands. "Definitely some beading happening here, Miss Annie."

But talking was fast becoming a problem. Craig bent down and captured one hardened nipple in his mouth, while his hands roamed restlessly down her leg.

NOTHING HAD EVER felt so right than holding Annie, worshipping her body. He couldn't promise her forever, but he could wipe away every negative thing her ex had her believe about herself.

"You are so beautiful," he whispered, trying to pull her on to his lap.

Gulping in air, she swung her leg over him and straddled him. Her gorgeous breasts were right in front of his eyes. Nearly reverently, he bent down to worship one, then the other, his own desire slowly spiraling out of control.

Only when her flesh was nearly burning his lips, her body pliant, did he lift his head. With unsteady fingers, he fastened her top at the back of her neck again. "I want you, Annie, but not here where your brother can storm in at any minute. If I book a room at the hotel, will you…"

Groaning, Annie stood up. "You ask me now when I can't think straight?"

Grinning, he also got up. "I love how honest you are about your feelings."

"I hate dancing around the topic."

"So is that a yes?"

"I have to think about, okay?"

He pulled her close. "All this thinking, seriously? I can kiss you until you decide?"

"Yeah, you can, but…"

"You feel what you do to me?" He stepped in between her legs.

"The throbbing?" she groaned. "How am I supposed to sleep tonight?"

"See? What you've just said. It makes me ache for you, Annie."

Her hand slid down his body. "Will it help if I touch it?" Her hand stroked his crotch, but he quickly grabbed her fingers.

"If you do that, I'm never leaving here tonight. Walk me out?"

With his blood still roaring in his ears, he took her hand and walked toward the door. She didn't say anything as they moved down the corridor.

He had to lighten the mood and fast, otherwise he might just pick her up and climb the stairs to her room—the brother be damned. "I've had another phone call to ask for help with marketing earlier."

"As far as I know, there isn't really someone in town who does that kind of thing, but you're leaving soon."

"Doesn't mean I can't help. Nowadays, you can work from any place."

"Of course, you could help them when you're back in Portland, but wouldn't you be too busy with your own work?"

Grimacing, he turned toward her. She was so damn beautiful, he had a hard time not bending down and kissing her again. "Problem is, I don't know if I want to do the work back in Portland anymore."

Annie raised her brows. "I thought you love your job. According to your aunt and Aiden, you're the hotshot at the firm."

"I've enjoyed it, but lately … I don't know. The last account we've won, had left a bitter taste in my mouth. Our idea was the better one, but the fact that our competitors lost to us made it impossible for them to continue. They had to close down, everyone there lost their jobs. I struggle not to think about that."

"You have such a big heart. I can understand how that would upset you."

A big heart? That wasn't how he was described back in Portland. There he was the cool and calculated one. And what the hell was he doing telling Annie about his problems? She had enough worries of her own. "Sorry, I didn't want to burden you with my issues. I'll pick you up at seven tomorrow night?"

"I'm here, if you want to talk, okay?"

He shook his head. "Thanks, but we have so little time together, I'm not wasting it moaning about my life."

"We're also friends, I hope. What about your parents? Don't you rather want to spend time with them?"

"I'll probably see them tomorrow. But tomorrow night, you and I have a date."

She pressed his hand. "You should talk to them, tell them how you feel, how you've been feeling. I know things are strained between you. Why they did what they did will probably always baffle you, but they're your parents and life is very short. I'd do anything to have another moment with mine."

Her words kept him thinking all the way back to Aunt Janice's house.

Chapter Thirteen

THE NEXT MORNING, Annie burned the croissants. Fed up, she stared at the nearly blackened blobs on the tray. Seriously. The reason? Another night of rolling around, aching for Craig. He'd lit a fire in her last night, one that not even a cold shower could extinguish. Whatever was she to do?

He could book a room at the hotel, he'd said. And that was the thought that had kept the beetles going round and round in her brain all night long.

There were ten days left before the wedding. Ten days. Would sleeping once with Craig be enough to quench this overwhelming thirst to be with him? Maybe she should throw caution to the wind and just go have sex with him in the hotel room—her whole being was spurring her on to do that. Carol Bingley would have a field day.

Just thinking about Craig woke up the butterflies. Groaning, she looked down at her nipples. And look at those two—beading again.

Muttering, she put another batch of croissants in the oven. This time she was going to stand right here and watch them.

"Talking to yourself again, Annie? Beetles busy?" Vivian chuckled from behind. She sniffed in the air. "Don't tell me you've burnt something again?"

"The croissants."

"Anything to do with the reason why you were so quiet last night? Riley told me Craig's parents will be arriving today. Apparently not something he'd mentioned to you?"

"He doesn't share his feelings easily." Annie shrugged. "It's okay, there's no reason for him to tell me anything about himself."

"Except for the fact that he can't seem to keep his hands to himself around you."

Annie bent to peer into the oven. "It's a temporary thing."

"Trying to convince me or yourself?"

"Oh, Viv, this isn't going anywhere. You know why I don't want to marry…"

"Actually, I don't. Ted was an idiot and didn't deserve you. You can't decide not to ever marry because one guy broke off your engagement weeks before the wedding. Besides, I don't remember you being very excited about marrying him anyway."

"Okay, I've come to realize I never really loved him, not like…" She swallowed the next words just in time. Like she loved Craig. Where did that come from? It wasn't true. The only thing between her and Craig was lust. Pure and simple.

"What I mean is, he was more like a brother to me. There was no spark."

"Well, there are definitely sparks, vibes, whatever you want to call it, between you and Craig. Those the kind of sparks you're talking about?"

"It doesn't matter. Even if, at some point, I will consider getting married again, it won't be to Craig. He's very adamant about not wanting to marry."

"You'll remember neither Aiden nor I wanted to get married, but then he came to Marietta and … well, we're getting married in ten days. Does Craig have a reason?"

Annie took the croissants out of the oven. "I've asked him. He said it probably had to do with the fact his parents left him with Aiden and Riley's parents when he was ten. Can you imagine?"

Vivian took a croissant from the tray. "The right woman may just change his mind. I have to go. But, Annie?"

"Yeah?"

"I think you're halfway in love with him already. Remember Mom's words? The ones you quoted to me not so long ago? You need to get out of your mind and into your heart. You've been so busy deciding not to marry again, you're missing what's in your heart. See you tonight!" Vivian left with a wave.

Irritated, Annie stared after her sister. Of course, she wasn't falling in love with Craig. They were having some fun, that was it.

Her phone bleeped. It was a text from Craig. Her heart bounced around happily in her chest just seeing his name. All he'd sent, though, was a link to her website.

Eagerly, she clicked on it and quickly scrolled down. Wow—it looked amazing. Craig had already added some of the new photos from Riley's shoot yesterday. Oh, this was so nice!

Her phone rang. It wasn't a number she knew. Maybe the call was from a potential customer, you never know. Rolling her eyes to her own silly thoughts, she answered the call.

Minutes later, she did a happy dance. She had more visitors for the Spring Arts and Crafts Festival. Whatever Craig had been doing was working wonders for traffic to the website of her small B and B. Annie's might just survive after all.

Mitch and Vivian had already left, Aiden was probably at the house, there was no one she could share her joy with. She desperately wanted to call Craig and tell him, but he wasn't going to be around forever. Oh, but she really, really wanted to tell him.

The clock on the oven pinged. The second batch of croissants was ready. *Focus, Annie, focus.* She'd send him a message, but first things first. The kitchen was a mess. She needed to clean it before she could do anything else.

Around eleven, the kitchen was sparkling. She was taking out her phone to finally send Craig a message when the doorbell rang. Dropping her phone in her pocket, she just about skipped to the front door. It could be Riley, although she'd said later today. In Marietta people didn't always wait for an invitation. Whoever it was, she had good news she'd love to share over a cup of tea.

With a big, welcoming smile, she opened the door. And froze. The man standing on her doorstep was the very last person she'd expected to ever see again. Ted. The same Ted who'd sent her a message weeks before their wedding day to break off their engagement.

"*Aah*, Annie," he said, stepping closer to grab her hands in his. "I've missed that smile. I've missed everything about you."

Stunned, she watched his head bending down to kiss her. Just before he could pull her closer, she finally got her voice back. "What are you doing here, Ted?"

CRAIG WAS DRIVING down Court Street on his way to town. He had an appointment to meet the owner of a new deli who also wanted to talk to him about marketing. The sixth shop owner asking for help.

Halfway down the street, he made a U-turn. He'd just had breakfast with his parents. The need to see Annie was too overwhelming to ignore. She was all he'd been thinking about since leaving Bramble House. There was still time before his next meeting. Her mere presence would calm his thoughts.

Driving slowly down Bramble Lane, he tried to quiet the storm raging in his chest. He didn't know what to think, how to make sense of the conversation his parents just had with him. Or rather, the conversation they didn't have with him.

He was turning to park in the driveway of Annie's house, when his foot hit the brakes. A strange car was parked in the street and right on her doorstep, for all to see some man was bending down to kiss Annie. What the hell?

He was out of the car and walking toward them before he'd taken the conscious decision to do so.

"What are you doing here, Ted?" said Annie's voice.

Craig hung back. Ted. Wasn't that the idiot who'd broke up with her weeks before their wedding day?

"I'm back, Annie, and I want to marry you. This time for real."

"I thought you didn't like a woman who only wants to cook and stay at home."

"But now you have a business!" he said, gesturing toward the house. "You have a professional website which tells me you must be doing well. With my construction skills, we can build this place up, hire someone as a chef, and sell franchises all over Montana. I'm so impressed by the website."

"I don't even know what to say to you, Ted. You never wanted me to have my own B and B. Please go."

He grabbed her arms. Craig saw red. Stepping forward, he put a hand on the man's shoulder. "Annie has asked you to go."

Ted turned around quickly, his eyes wary. But Craig was obviously not who he'd been worried about seeing and he smiled again. "I don't know who you are, but Annie here is my fiancée."

With a frown, Craig turned toward Annie. *What the hell?* "I didn't know you were still engaged."

"Well, now you do," Ted said, putting a hand on Annie's arm.

Annie pulled away quickly and hands on hips, her eyes mere slits, she turned to Ted. "I am not engaged to you or anyone, nor do I plan to ever be engaged again. Please leave."

Ted's face had turned red. "If I leave now, I'm not ever coming back."

"Great," Annie said. "This is my house, my business, my B and B, and I love being the chef, thank you very much."

"Think about it," Ted said. "I don't know if you'll get a better offer in this little town." And turning away he walked back to his car.

Craig put out a hand to touch her, but she was clearly not in the mood.

"And you," she said, "I am quite capable of fighting my own battles, thank you very much."

"I know." He chuckled. "You were magnificent."

Behind them, Ted's car sped away with tires screeching.

For a moment longer, she glared at him, but then she burst out laughing. "Sorry, I'm probably more rattled than I've realized. I couldn't believe my eyes. Ted at my front door."

"So, you don't want him back?"

Annie rolled her eyes. "No, I don't want him back. You know why he's here?"

"Because he realized what an idiot he's been?"

"Because of you."

"Me?"

"With your marketing skills, you've succeeded in putting Annie's on the map. I've had more potential visitors phoning all morning. Apparently, even Ted has found Annie's website. Having my own B and B has always been my dream, but he never liked the idea, so I didn't give it another thought. Now he thinks I'm very successful because of the nice website. Thought he could waltz right back into my life."

"Well, good riddance."

Annie cocked her head. "Another question is why are you here? Our date is only tonight, isn't it?"

"It is, but I needed to see you."

"Oh? You want to cancel the date? Because if you've changed your mind, that's totally okay. The whole thing is ridiculous, anyway, you're leaving soon and—"

Before she could finish her sentence, he'd pulled her closer and cut off the rest of her words with a kiss. It was only supposed to shut her up, but he should've known just a taste of Annie's lips was never enough.

With a sigh, her lips parted, his tongue found its way into the warm, welcoming depths of her mouth and he was lost. The noise of his blood roaring through his body silenced all other sounds, and it was only when Annie lifted her head that he heard his phone ringing.

"Damn, woman, you make me forget everything else," he whispered against her lips. "I have an appointment..." He quickly took out his ringing phone from his pocket.

Annie's eyes dropped to his phone. "With ... Sandra? Sorry," she said, stepping back into her house. "I didn't mean to look. Enjoy your date!"

"It's not a date, damn it, Annie..." His phone had finally stopped ringing. "She's opened a new deli in town and wants to talk about marketing."

"Oh, that Sandra," Annie said, chewing her lip, her big brown eyes looking worried. "She's gorgeous."

"Jealous?"

"I'm taking the Fifth," she said primly, crossing her arms.

Laughing, he pulled her closer and kissed her soundly. "You, Annie, have nothing to be jealous about. I can't think straight because of you, let alone look at another woman. See you tonight!"

She grabbed his arm. "Wait. Have you seen your parents?"

He nodded. "I've seen them. They talked about the

house, what their plans are, you know, the usual things."

"You didn't talk about … you know? Feelings? Why they've left you all those years ago?"

"Talking about feelings and explaining things are not topics we're comfortable discussing."

"I'd thought they would at least try and explain their reasoning?"

He shrugged. "They probably don't think they need to say anything. And maybe they're right. Nothing they do or say can change what has happened." He grimaced "They did invite me to go with them to Yellowstone National Park. What on earth for? I don't have anything to say to them." But standing so close to Annie, he didn't want to talk about his parents. He bent down for another kiss. "See you tonight."

"Can't wait." She smiled. "Oh, and I've posted on Instagram this morning. My video is not as professional as the photos Riley has posted, but I'm willing to give it a go."

"And? Any reaction?"

"I haven't checked, probably not. I've followed a few foodies as Riley had suggested, but I have the sum total of two followers when I posted the video."

"Let's see," he insisted.

"We can do it later…" she began but he kept holding out his hand. "Okay, but…"

Ignoring her, he opened the Insta icon and watched the two-minute video with her where she explained the basics of making scones. "This is great, Annie."

"You think so?"

"I know so. How many followers did you say you have?"

"Two…"

"Well, you now have five hundred and look here…" He showed her how to check insights into her post. "If you click on this, you see what kind of traffic your post generated. Wow, four hundred people viewed your video. Some of those you followed shared your video and your hashtag #annieisbaking seems to have been repeated a number of times." He handed back her phone. "You're good at this, Annie. As I've told you, you are the brand, the secret to Annie's success. You just may start trending one of these days."

Her brilliant smile stayed with him until he parked in front of Java Café where he was supposed to meet his potential client. As he got out of his car, he chuckled. He still had a stupid grin on his face in spite of the disappointing breakfast he'd had with his parents.

The tightness around his chest had eased a bit. Annie could do that with her warm smile and sweet kisses.

Chapter Fourteen

LATE AFTERNOON, MITCH stormed into Annie's kitchen, eyes blazing. "Is it true?"

Rubbing her temple, Annie sighed. All this shouting was getting to her. "What now? Is what true?"

"That Ted freaking Harris knocked on your door this morning?"

Stunned, Annie stared at Mitch. "How on earth do you know that?"

"Marcus Baker, the science teacher, who is always asking about you? Well, he had coffee at the diner before school this morning where he ran into Carol Bingley. He wanted to know from me why you haven't told anyone you're still engaged."

"Of course, I'm not engaged to him…"

"And why was Craig O'Sullivan kissing you at the front door for everyone to see?"

Annie had had enough. "Seriously, Mitch, this is getting so old. We like kissing each other. In fact, I may just sleep with him before he goes back to Portland."

Mitch turned red, his mouth opened and closed, but no

sound came out, thank goodness.

Quickly, she touched his arm. "I appreciate you looking out for me, Mitch, but I do this with eyes wide open. I don't want to get married again, but I enjoy being with Craig. He's been very honest right from the start. He has his own reasons for not wanting to ever tie the knot and I'm not expecting anything. Also, because of his help with my website, I've been getting more and more bookings during the day, all visitors who'll be here for next weekend's Spring Arts and Crafts Festival. So, for the next few days, he and I will be together."

"And what happens when he leaves, Annie? I know you. You have feelings for him, he's going to break your heart."

At least her brother had stopped shouting. "Hearts break, brother dear, they also heal. Stop growling and be happy for me, please? Craig is picking me up at seven, we're going on a date, and you are not going to shout, okay?"

Mitch's frown only deepened. "I don't like it. What about the rest of the family when you two break up? Can you imagine how awkward family gatherings will be?"

"We're friends first, we'll go back to being friends, no awkward gatherings, I promise you. You don't have to like it, Mitch, but we are together for the moment. Come on, stop frowning. I've made your favorite—brandy-fried chicken. You can just heat it when you're hungry."

Finally, the corners of Mitch's mouth lifted ever so slightly. Hugging her, he sighed. "Thank you. You don't have to cook for me if you're going out. I don't mean to shout, it's just … I don't want you to get hurt again."

"I don't know what has gotten into you. You're my soft-spoken, always smiling brother."

"You and Viv are my family. I have to look out for you."

She hugged him. "And I love you for it, I really do. But all this shouting can't be good for you. Is there something else going on I should know about?" Staring at her brother, she grinned. "Don't tell me all this huffing and puffing has to do with a woman? Who is she?"

"Don't be ridiculous. I can promise you that's the very last thing on my mind."

"Your novel then. How is the writing going?"

Sighing, Mitch rubbed his face. "It's not going. Probably the main reason for my frustration."

"You'll need to sit down in front of your computer if you actually want to write. I haven't seen you do that in a while."

"Well, I've been worried about Vivian and now you…"

Grinning, Annie leaned against him for a moment. "I'll be okay. And now I'm going to have a shower and put on my dancing shoes."

She was halfway up the stairs when she heard Mitch's voice again. "I still don't like it!"

Rolling her eyes, Annie hurried to her room.

She knew exactly what she'd be wearing tonight. Craig was not going to be able to keep his hands to himself.

CRAIG WENT LOOKING for his aunt before he left to pick up Annie. She was in the kitchen with Riley and Dylan.

"It smells nice in here." He smiled as he entered.

"We're making hamburgers," Dylan announced.

"Don't you look handsome," his aunt said, giving him a once-over. "You have a date with Annie?"

"Yes, we're trying Grey's Saloon tonight."

"I'm surprised she's going with you. There's a story going around Annie's fiancé pitched up to claim her again. Carol Bingley heard from—"

"That's nonsense," Craig interrupted. "He showed up on her doorstep, yes, but she doesn't want him back."

Riley chuckled. "You have been busy this morning. I heard you kissed Annie right there in front of her door. What I want to know is whether that was before or after her ex-fiancé showed up? And when did you have time to take Sandra from the deli for coffee? Everyone is talking about that as well. Apparently, there is a wager going on in town— who is the woman you've bought the boxes of you-know-what for? And, of course, everyone knows you've booked a room at the hotel for tonight."

Stunned, Craig stared at his sister. "What the—"

Riley quickly motioned toward Dylan and Craig swallowed the swear word.

"I don't believe it. I was with Annie for all of ten

minutes. And Sandra is one of six … or seven new clients I now have."

Aunt Janice patted his arm. "Small towns. Everything you do, or not do, is noticed. Let me walk you out."

At the door, she gave him a hug. "We haven't had a chance to talk. Have you seen your parents?"

He nodded. "I have."

"And?"

"Nothing. They asked how I am, told me how they're doing. That was about it. I have to go now. I don't want to be late." He kissed her cheek before he stepped out.

"You're leaving soon. Annie is staying," his aunt said as he turned away to walk to his car.

He stopped. "We both know this is only temporary."

"If you say so. It's just … you're going back to Portland, but she'll still be here. Whatever rumors are doing the rounds will be something she'll have to deal with on her own."

Nodding, he walked toward his car. He knew exactly what his aunt wasn't saying. Irritated, he got into his car.

The room he'd booked at the hotel would have to be canceled. Tomorrow there'd probably be another story, another wager.

ANNIE STOLE A glimpse at Craig as he parked the car in front of Grey's Saloon. Her mouth had literally begun to water when she'd seen him. Dressed in a crisp white shirt and jeans, he was devastatingly attractive.

He'd been quiet all the way. His eyes had darkened as she came down the stairs. She'd hoped the white dress with maroon polka dots that crossed over her breasts, would elicit some reaction, but she wasn't prepared for the flash of heat in his eyes or the way his gaze had raked over her. The dress had long sleeves, the neck was wide, leaving her shoulders bare. With it, she wore another pair of hoop earrings.

He hadn't said anything, just let his fingers trail across her back as he'd helped her into her coat. He'd taken her hand as he drove away from her house, but he hadn't said a word since.

With her hand on the door, she turned to him. "What is wrong, Craig? And don't tell me nothing, I know you. I told you if you don't want to do this, it's fine. I'll probably be sad when you leave, but I'll get over it in time. What I don't want is for you to do something you don't want to..."

His arms shot out and he just about hauled her on to his lap before she'd finished speaking.

With unsteady fingers, he stroked her shoulders before his hand glided down to follow the neckline of her dress, just above her breasts. "Do you have any idea what you do to me? You are so, so beautiful, I ache for you. I've booked a room in the hotel tonight but apparently, the whole damn town is talking about us, so I've cancelled it again. I don't want people talking about you."

"There are rumors about you and the lovely Sandra doing the rounds as well."

Groaning, he cupped her face. "You've heard about that too?"

"I have. Apparently, she couldn't stop touching you."

"Did she? I don't remember. I was thinking about you the whole time." Inhaling deeply, he closed his eyes for a moment. "Damn it, Annie, I don't want to hurt you. I wasn't expecting people to talk, to gossip about you, about us. I'm leaving, but you'll be staying behind…"

Annie moved back to her seat. She knew what needed to be done. "This is getting way more complicated than either of us had anticipated. Let's chalk the whole thing up to hormones and strange times. It'll pass. Let's have dinner as friends, talk about happy things, and afterward go our merry ways. We'll probably see one another at the wedding, but by then this craziness would've subsided."

"That's not …"

Her heart breaking into a million little pieces, she opened the door. "Come on, friend, I'm hungry."

"YOU SHOULDN'T EXPECT much," Annie was babbling away as they walked toward Grey's saloon. "Grey's Saloon is something right out of an old cowboy movie. Apparently, it's the oldest building in town. I don't think the battered bar, the booths, or the scarred floorboards have ever been replaced."

It was difficult following what Annie was saying, Craig was gnashing his teeth together, trying his best not to touch Annie. She was right. He didn't like it, but everything she'd said, made sense. It was better for both of them if he didn't see her again after tonight.

As they entered, a tall guy ahead of them spotted Annie and, with a huge grin, he stepped closer to her. It was the cowboy she'd been on a date with.

"Hi, Annie, how lovely to see you. Give me a call. I think it's time for our second date."

"Thanks, Hunter…" Annie began, but without thinking, Craig put an arm around Annie's shoulders.

The guy winked at Annie. "When he leaves. I'm not going anywhere and am happy to wait for you."

Fed up with the whole scenario, Craig took Annie's hand. This was ridiculous.

Annie tried to pull her hand from his, but he wouldn't let go. "Craig, friends don't walk hand in hand."

"I have to touch you, damn it," he growled as they walked toward the counter. "I don't like that guy."

"You don't know him. He's very nice."

As they walked toward an open table, Craig kept Annie close to his side. "I don't want to think about you with someone else."

Annie smiled wryly. "Good. Then you know how I feel about you going back to dating two women at a time."

Dating two women? He didn't want to date anyone else, let alone two women at the same time.

All along the way, people got up to greet Annie. It was difficult not to notice the side looks in his direction and the whispering. One thing was clear—just about everybody in town had heard the rumors.

As they were about to sit down at their table, someone called his name. When he looked behind him, his parents were sitting at a table close by. For a moment, he considered grabbing Annie's hand and leaving.

"Craig, do you know those people?" Annie asked.

"My parents."

"But then we have to sit with them, come on." Taking his hand, she walked over to where his parents were sitting.

His dad got up as they neared. "Craig," he said, smiling uncertainly.

His mother's eyes had zoomed in on his hand around Annie's.

"Mr. and Mrs. O'Sullivan, it's so nice to meet you," Annie said, her beautiful smile in place.

"Mom, Dad, this is Annie Miller."

Smiling, his mother also got up and shook hands with Annie. "Miller? Are you related to Vivian who is marrying Aiden?"

"Yes, she's my sister." Annie smiled.

"Won't you join us?" his dad asked.

Craig opened his mouth to decline, but Annie was already pulling out a chair. "Thank you, how kind."

Reluctantly, Craig sat down next to Annie. This was so not what he'd had in mind for this evening. He and Annie were going to have dinner and wine. Afterward, he'd planned to take her to the room at the hotel where he'd take his time getting her naked before he would've made love to her until the sun rose.

The reality couldn't be more different. Having dinner with his parents—with just about half the town as nosy onlookers to boot—was so not his idea of a hot date.

APPARENTLY, CRAIG'S PARENTS had also just arrived at the saloon and hadn't ordered yet. The next few minutes were spent deciding on what to eat and what to drink. The waiter finally left, leaving a slightly awkward silence behind.

Craig was looking at his hands, his dad was staring at the roof. Seriously, didn't this family talk to one another?

Catching Craig's mom's eye, Annie smiled. Well, she was not going to be quiet. "Mrs. O'Sullivan, Craig tells you've been with Doctors Without Borders since he was ten?"

Craig's mother smiled. "Please call me Claire and my husband is Robert. We've always been drawn to help those in need. As students, we volunteered to help out where needed. When Craig was ten, we were once more made aware of the need of so many people all over the world. At the time, Rwandan refugees were dying in Kisangani, in Colombia thousands were displaced, Georgian refugees wanted to return home, to name but a few. Doctors Without Borders were looking for people to help in these parts. Robert's brother Sean and his wife offered to have Craig stay with them while we were away, making it possible for us to go and help where we could. So that's what we did."

The waiter arrived, and while he handed everyone a drink, Annie looked at Craig. His jaws were clenched together, his hands restlessly rubbing his legs. Without conscious thought, Annie reached out and touched him. Craig grabbed her hand as if she was his lifeline.

"Wasn't it hard for you?" Annie asked Craig's mom. "At ten, my world revolved around my parents. They were the people who made me feel safe. I can't imagine a childhood without their support and love."

Shaking her head, Craig's mom smiled. "We've raised Craig to be independent. We knew he was happy and well looked after. Sean and Cara raised him as their own son. We saw him during our off times, but his timetable became so busy and we were away for long periods of time. But now that we've retired, we're hoping we can spend more time together."

Craig's dad cleared his throat. "Yes, we're on our way to

Yellowstone National Park and we're hoping to persuade Craig to come with us. It would only be for a few days, we'll be back for Aiden's wedding."

"You've been invited?" Craig asked.

"Well, yes, we're family," his mom said.

Next to her, Craig exhaled slowly. "I hope you enjoy your trip, I won't be joining you. Going to Yellowstone National Park is one of those things I would've loved to do when I was ten."

Both his parents looked perplexed. Fortunately, the waiter arrived with their food at that precise moment.

Annie looked at the three people with her around the table. *What's wrong with them?* She could bang their heads together. *Why don't they just talk to one another?* Surely, if Craig could share his feelings with them, they'd know how hurt and scared he'd been.

Picking up her knife and fork, Annie inhaled deeply. Not her business. They'd sort out their own problems. Besides, after tonight, she wouldn't see Craig again except at the wedding.

TRYING TO SWALLOW his food was a huge effort and after a few bites, Craig put down his knife and fork. Fortunately, Annie was chattering away about the upcoming spring festival.

He put an arm around her chair, making sure his fingers touched her shoulders. She was the only reason why he hadn't already left.

"Will be held at the fairgrounds outside town," Annie was saying. "The same place where the rodeos also take place. It's an arts and crafts festival with lots of stalls with food. There's also live music. My brother and sister and I moved to Marietta about a year ago and the festival was the first event we attended. Lots of fun."

"First event?" his mother asked, clearly amused. "Are there many other events?"

"Oh, yes." Annie smiled. "In summer we have the Marietta fair, homecoming is usually a whole weekend of festivities. There is also a bachelor auction at some point and around Christmas there are all sorts of things happening in and around our town."

"We've been all over the world," his mother said, "but now that we've retired, I want to be in a city. I could never settle in a small town for good. I like to be near shops and theaters and an airport. I can't see you living in a small town either, Craig."

"But then you don't know me at all, do you, Mother?" The moment the words were out, he wished he'd kept his mouth shut, but he couldn't sit here a moment longer, pretending everything was okay.

"Are you ready to leave?" he asked Annie as he took out his wallet.

She gave him one look before she got up. "It was lovely to meet you," she said to his parents. "When you have time, do stop at Annie's for a cup of tea."

Craig put money on the table and nodded in the direction of his parents. "Good night." Without looking back, he took Annie's hand and made a beeline for the door.

Chapter Fifteen

As CRAIG STOPPED in front of her house, Annie tried to pull her hand out of his, but he held on tightly.

He pressed her fingers to his mouth, his eyes glowing with a light that made her glad she was sitting down. "I'm not ready to say goodbye. May I please come in?"

Annie stared at him, the beetles in her head doing some serious jumping around. This was such a bad idea, logic tried to reason, but heart won, hands down. She didn't want to say goodbye either. "Of course."

He jumped out and was opening her door before she could get out of the car. Lacing their fingers, he walked her to the front door. It was still early, but hopefully Mitch and Aiden and Vivian would already be in their rooms.

"You want coffee or a drink?" she asked as she closed the front door behind them.

He shook his head. "Does the door to your office lock?"

"Yes, it does," she answered all the other questions he wasn't asking. Dropping her jacket on the chair, she followed him down the corridor.

Craig entered the office before her, she locked the door

behind her. Not quite sure what to expect next, she leaned back against it.

Hands in pockets, Craig stepped closer. "I want to be with you, Annie. I have no right to ask you and if you'd rather—"

This time, she was the one to shut him up with a kiss. Raising herself on her toes, her arms crept around his neck. She kissed him with all the pent-up desire that had been building up over the last few days.

Within seconds, she was ready to go up in flames. Tongues met in a desperate dance. There was only this one night.

Without taking his mouth from hers, Craig picked her up. As if they'd done this a hundred times before, her legs closed around his body as he staggered toward the couch.

Even like this, plastered against him, she couldn't get enough. She was never going to get enough of this man and his kisses. Slowly, he let her slide down his body, reveling in every soft curve touching him. Only then did he lift his head.

His eyes were mere slits, his breathing ragged. "What you do to me with just a kiss, Miss Annie," he got out before he bent down and feasted on her shoulder. "This was all I've been thinking about tonight. Being with you, like this. Tasting you…" His hand slid the neckline of her dress farther down, his mouth following right behind his fingers. Restlessly, he pulled at her dress. "How do I get rid of this thing?"

"There's … there's a button." She gasped.

He lifted his head. "A button? Just one?"

"Yes, just here…" She showed him.

Cussing softly, he undid the button. "Damn, it's a good thing I didn't know that." With his eyes on hers, he opened the button, his fingers just grazing her skin. Noiselessly, the dress slid to the floor.

His eyes darkened as they roamed over her body. "Pink lace. I'll always think of you in pink lace. Beautiful Annie," he whispered as his hands cupped her breasts. "I've been dreaming about being with you like this from the first time I saw you." With a groan, he captured her lips with his again.

As she gave herself up to him, her hands slid beneath his shirt, reveling in his toned body, his warm flesh. But she wanted more.

"I think you're overdressed," she whispered against his lips as her fingers tried to unbutton his shirt.

Cussing softly, he pulled his shirt over his head in one movement and let it drop to floor.

"Oh, my." She sighed, letting her hands spread over the muscles in front of her. "I've dreamt about this, too," she whispered as she bent down to taste him.

THE SOFT SOUNDS from Annie's throat were driving him wild. He wasn't going to last much longer. He'd been hard for her since he'd walked onto her porch to see her touching her breasts. Only days ago, but it felt like a lifetime had passed.

He'd seen her breasts before, had touched them, but this was different. He wanted her like he'd never wanted anyone before. His body had been ready for her, but the pink lace bra and triangle had sent his blood to boiling within seconds.

His hands roamed over her body, touching every soft curve, relishing in her softness, drinking in her unique scent. He was never going to get enough of this woman.

"Look at me, Annie. I want to see your eyes when I touch you," he murmured.

Her eyes, when she looked up at him, were feverish, darkened with passion. Completely captivated by her, he ran his hand down her body and back before he unhooked her bra. "I've dreamt about these," he murmured, watching her eyes glaze over.

In awe, he touched her breasts. The whimpering sound she made shot right down to the soles of his feet. The couch was going to be way too small for what he had in mind.

Easing Annie down to the carpet, he quickly got rid of his pants before he joined her. Leaning on his elbow, he crushed his mouth to hers. Slender arms circled his neck as he teased and loved her lips.

Only when her body moved restlessly beneath him, did he let his lips travel down her face, along her neck, down to her breasts where he lingered, savored, tortured. Her soft hands stroked his back, their legs tangled together.

He wanted to give her everything he could. They'd have this one night. It would have to be enough.

SHE HADN'T KNOWN it was possible to feel so much. Nobody's touch had ever elicited so much joy, so many overpowering sensations. All her senses were stimulated to a point where she was worried she'd burst into flames.

Big hands were stroking her flesh, lips were slowly moving down her body, inch by delicious inch. Murmuring soft words she couldn't quite make out, Craig explored her body thoroughly while his mouth continued its journey downward.

The need to become a part of him was making her delirious. She pleaded and sobbed, her body arching up, wanting more. Finally, his mouth closed around her heat, stars exploded behind her eyelids, a wild wind picked her up, tossed her deep into a stormy sea where waves of pleasure tumbled relentlessly over her.

WATCHING HER CREST, he stroked her smooth skin, moist from their lovemaking. Somewhere inside him, something that had been wound tightly for a long time loosened.

He didn't let her catch her breath but used his hands and mouth to slowly drive her up and up until her sighs turned to gasps. And then he brought her over the edge again. Only when he was sure she was ready, when she was pliant in his arms and whimpering his name, her body arching up to him, did he move over her.

Inch by delicious inch, he slid into her, her warmth welcoming him. Finally. He was where he'd been dreaming about for so long, where he was meant to be. Bending down, he caught her eager lips. Long, silky legs slipped around him, pulling him closer. Gripping her hands tightly, he lifted his head as he began to move.

And as if they'd had this dance a thousand times before, she quickly found his rhythm, her eyes locked with his as they surged forward together.

Desperate not to miss a thing, he tried watching her, he wanted to remember every single detail about her, but with his blood roaring in his ears, his heart beating in sync with hers, his head fell backward as they rode the next wave together.

He'd never made love like this—his last rational thought before he shouted Annie's name.

ANNIE OPENED HER eyes. She was lying on top of a very nice, warm body. In the next minute, though, pleasure was replaced with sadness clutching at her throat. It had to end. He had to go, but for one more minute, she was going to enjoy being here with him like this.

Everything was different. She was different. She'd made love with Craig. He'd made love to her.

Love. Just four letters.

Her heart skipped a beat, she closed her eyes, swallowing the groan in her throat. Damn. She'd gone and fallen in love with him. It probably happened the first time he and Riley had visited and he'd pulled her into a hug.

How could she have known then what her heart had been trying to tell her?

It hadn't been lust at all ... well, okay, of course lust had to take some blame, but that wasn't the only thing she'd experienced in Craig's arms over the last few hours.

Time and time again, he'd woken her up, ready for her, and each time she'd eagerly turned to him. They only had the one night. They would be able to walk away afterward, the itch scratched, the beading and the throbbing finally sated.

She looked down at their tangled limbs. However, the beading and the throbbing were very much still happening. Only now she understood why. She loved him. Her body had known it way before her heart was ready to acknowledge it. And it wasn't a love that one night with Craig would be able to still or stop. It was the forever kind.

Turning her head, she pressed her lips against his warm

flesh, inhaling his scent. She would always be grateful for this night. She hadn't known what love was until he'd showed her all the ways there were to love.

A movement against her leg, made her smile. Her lover was awake.

ANNIE WALKED HIM to the front door. She was quiet. It was just after five in the morning and still dark outside. He'd have given anything to have stayed with her for one more hour, but he had nothing to offer her. He had to leave. Say goodbye. The next time he would see her, they'd just be friends.

She unlocked the front door, he stepped out on to the porch before he turned back to her. "Annie..."

Shaking her head, she touched his face. "We've said all there is to say. Thank you for all your help with the B and B and thank you for last night. I hope you'll be happy. Talk to your parents, tell them how you feel, discuss your feelings, however uncomfortable. You don't know how long they'll still be around."

"Riley told me how your parents died. I'm so sorry about that."

She nodded. "Life is so very short. You deserve the best, Craig. You deserve to marry, have lots of kids, and make some woman happy." The door began to close.

Quickly, he stopped the door. "One more kiss?"

Her eyes were bright with tears as she opened the door wider.

"You're crying."

"My heart is breaking," she got out before his lips closed over hers.

And immediately the fire was back. Slipping his hand into the front of her dress, he cupped her breast, kissing her until she shuddered against his body.

Only then he lifted his head. "Beautiful Annie," he whispered, caressing her cheek.

Annie swallowed, her eyes roaming over his face. "Goodbye, Craig." She stepped back and, without looking at him again, closed the door.

Pressing his forehead against the door, he waited for her footsteps. Around him, sounds penetrated. The day had started, people were going about their usual morning routines while his heart was breaking.

After a while, he turned away and walked to the road in front of Annie's. He was doing the right thing. Annie might not know it yet, but she deserved a husband. She'd be a great mom. As a natural nurturer and caretaker, her kids would never have to wonder if their mom loved them, they'd know.

Little girls with their mother's big, brown eyes, her smile, his light red hair. For a moment the picture was so clear, he could touch it. He blinked and it was gone. It wasn't real, though.

Looking over his shoulder once last time, he got into the car. A hole opened up inside of him, one that grew bigger and deeper as he drove away from Annie's front door.

He needed a drink. Surely even a town as small as Marietta would have a bar that was open at all hours?

Chapter Sixteen

L ATE WEDNESDAY AFTERNOON, Annie stepped warily into the kitchen. She'd managed to avoid seeing her sister or brother since Craig had left early this morning, but at some point they'd want answers.

Craig, she'd discovered, might not talk much but he was a loud lover and she had an idea she hadn't been very quiet either. Although they'd been in her office on the ground floor, she was sure everyone in the house had probably heard something.

She was doing her best not to think about their lovemaking, a difficult task since everything in her office reminded her of last night. Every single line she'd ever read in a romance novel seemed to pop into her head the moment she walked in there.

Lingering kisses, hot flesh, ravishing her body and words like *succumbing, passion, plundering, surrendering* and her favorite? *Exploding.* She'd exploded quite a number of times, if memory served her right.

"There you are," Vivian said. She was sitting at the table, sipping her coffee. "I was wondering whether you were hiding from us."

Annie walked toward the coffee machine. "Why would I be hiding?"

Vivian chuckled. "I don't know. It may have something to do with the all the sounds coming from your office last night?"

"Sounds?"

"Oh, come on, Annie. It's me. Your sister. You've been with Craig?"

With a sigh, Annie took a seat at the table. "Yes, okay, I was with Craig. But it was a one-time only thing. I won't be seeing him again before he leaves. Well, except on your wedding day, of course. But that's more than a week away."

"You won't be seeing him again? Mmm, that would explain it." Vivian chuckled.

"Explain what?"

"The stiches he needed early this morning. Right here," Vivian said pointing to her chin.

Trying to process what Vivian's words meant, Annie put her mug down slowly. "Stiches? You mean Craig..." She couldn't even say the words. Inhaling deeply, she tried to focus on her sister, but everything around her seemed to be tilting.

Vivian nodded as she jumped up. "Yep, four or five if I remember correctly. Annie, are you okay? You're white as a sheet." She quickly got a bottle of water from the fridge and gave it to Annie.

Annie pressed the cold bottle against her face. "Why did he need stitches? What happened?"

"Apparently a fight broke out at the Wolf Den early this morning. It was a rough morning in the ER stitching up half the cowboys in town. Oh, and Ted Harris also staggered in."

"Ted? I didn't know he was still in town?" Nothing Vivian was saying made any sense.

"I have an idea he's finally realized he's not welcome here. Can't tell you how I enjoyed stitching him up. He looked the worse of the two, by the way."

"Craig—is he okay?"

Vivian grinned. "Don't worry, he'll live. At least now I understand how a grown man ended up in a fight in the seediest bar in town. If you told him you don't want to see him again, I'm starting to have a little sympathy for the man."

"Sympathy for what man?" Mitch asked as he entered the kitchen.

"Annie's Craig ended up in the ER this morning."

"Oh, the fight at the Wolf Den early this morning?" Mitch snickered. "Heard about it at school. Serves him right. Strutting in here, flirting with my sister."

Vivian chuckled. "Just please don't you also go and throw punches again. You've already been the talk of the town when you hit poor Aiden."

"He made you cry, or have you forgotten about that?"

Smiling, Vivian hugged Mitch. "I remember. What you

should remember, brother dear, is that you're a lover, not a fighter. Be nice with Craig. Even though he doesn't know it yet, he's fallen for our Annie. She, on the other hand, knows she loves him, but she's still determined never to marry because of that idiot Ted Harris, who by the way, was part of the fight. If you want to do something, talk to Annie, tell her she can't throw away a happy future because of silly person who doesn't know her worth."

Still dumbfounded, Annie watched as Vivian left the kitchen. Craig had been in the Wolf Den. He'd been in a fight right after he'd left her early this morning. With Ted. Like two little schoolboys. For heaven's sake—what had he been thinking?

Inhaling deeply, she pressed her fingers against her temples where the vague headache she'd been aware of all morning was now pounding away. Craig was okay. For a minute there she'd thought she was going to faint.

"Is it true?" Mitch asked as he pulled out a chair, mug of coffee in his one hand.

"Is what true?"

"That you love O'Sullivan?"

Sighing, Annie took a sip of the cold water. "Yes, Mitch, I do. I didn't know it was possible to love someone so, so … completely. Corny, I know, but that's how it is."

"Have you told him?"

"There's no point. He doesn't want to get married."

"What about you?"

"After Ted, I was so hurt. I'd thought if I protect my heart, I'll never feel that pain again." Grimacing, she picked up her mug. "Turns out, if the right person walks into your life, there isn't much you can do about it. The heart wants what the heart wants. To answer your question—I'll marry Craig in a heartbeat if he asks me, but it's not going to happen."

Mitch got up. "I, for one, am glad someone punched him. Saves me the trouble."

Touching his arm, Annie smiled. "I love you, too."

Still muttering, Mitch left the kitchen.

Annie picked up her phone. Seconds later, she put it down again. Vivian had said Craig was okay, but she wanted to make sure. Everything in her was urging her to phone him or send him a message to find out whether he was, in fact, okay. But... They'd agreed they wouldn't be seeing one another before he left, except for the wedding.

She could check with Janice, though. Surely that wouldn't count as contacting Craig?

BY THE TIME Craig walked into his aunt's kitchen, it was time for dinner. He'd finally fallen asleep around lunch.

Having Vivian, Annie's sister, stitch him up at the ER was not something he'd want to experience again. She'd been smiling way too widely for his peace of mind and seemed to thoroughly enjoy hurting him.

The only thing that had made the whole thing tolerable was seeing Ted Harris looking worse than he did. At least the fight had made sure Harris left town. When last he saw the guy, he was getting into a shuttle going to the airport from the hospital.

Grimacing, he tried to prepare himself for all the questions from his aunt and sister. He felt like an idiot. Damn it, he was an idiot. As he gingerly touched his chin, he again noticed his swollen fingers.

All he could think of was Annie. Damn, he missed her. He'd wanted to call her so many times since this morning, but he'd agreed with her they wouldn't see each other again before the wedding.

"Look what the cat dragged in, Aunt Janice," Riley drawled without a trace of sympathy.

Dylan was playing with his cars. When the little boy saw him, he jumped up. His eyes widened as he pointed at Craig's chin. "Ouchie?"

Riley chuckled. "Yes, sweetheart, that's an ouchie. It happens when you go looking for trouble."

Rushing forward, Dylan threw his arms around Craig's legs. "Is it better?"

Feeling like a fool, Craig patted Dylan's head. "I'm okay, but thanks for the sympathy. Not much of that going around, it seems."

Riley was still grinning. "He doesn't look too bad, Aunt

Janice, what do you say?"

Aunt Janice crossed her arms, her mouth pressed tightly together. Oh, man—he wasn't looking forward to this.

"I supposed you all know what happened?" he said as he pulled out the nearest chair.

His aunt pulled herself upright. "That my godson walked into the Wolf Den, of all places, at some ungodly hour and picked a fight with a stranger? Yes, I've heard that. Betty, the police dispatcher phoned Carol Bingley as soon as she heard the news and then, of course, Carol felt duty bound to tell as many people as possible in as short a time as possible."

"I didn't start it. Ted Harris, Annie's ex, was saying nasty things about her."

"So, you punched him?" Riley whispered. "What good will that do?"

"I shouldn't have done that, I'm sorry. But I couldn't sit by and let him talk about Annie like that."

"What time was this?" Riley asked.

"Early this morning."

"So, you got out of bed at that time and went to the Wolf Den to look for a fight?" his aunt asked.

"No, I didn't sleep here. I … I was with Annie last night. And then … well, long story short, we've decided not to see each other again before I leave. We'll both be at the wedding, of course. But just as friends."

By the time he'd finished talking, both women were staring at him, open-mouthed.

Aunt Janice was the first to speak. "Let me get this straight—you and Annie spent a night together but then you decided you're not going to see each other again? It doesn't make any sense. You obviously feel something for her and she's clearly mad about you."

"There are feelings, but neither one of us wants anything more permanent, like marriage. A clean break makes more sense at this point."

"So don't get married," Riley said. "It doesn't have to be all or nothing, seriously. Marriage isn't for everybody, definitely not for me, that's for sure. But it doesn't mean you can't be together for as long as you both want it."

"My life is in Portland."

"Is it, though?" Riley asked. "If I recall, you haven't been very happy over the last few months. And there are planes and trains and cars, remember? If memory serves me right, you've recently said, and I quote, 'life without traffic and deadlines sounds infinitely better than the reality back in the city.' You could always work from here."

"You already have quite a few clients in Marietta," his aunt added.

Riley wasn't finished either. "If you think about it, you're already working from here. Okay, yes, you don't go to an office, but you keep in touch with your team in Portland daily, you help out on a regular basis. As a bonus, you're getting new clients daily."

"I haven't worked…" he began but stopped.

His cousin was right. He had been working nonstop since he'd arrived in Marietta. Not only to help everyone who'd asked around here, but he'd also been helping his team back in Portland.

"See?" Riley smiled.

"I'm no good for Annie."

Aunt Janice groaned out loud. "That is not true and you know it. She lights up every time she sees you. And you're a completely different person when you're with her. More open, more tactile. You've never been a hugger, now you are. But, okay, if you don't want to be with her, so be it. I know of a number of men who would be very happy to hear you and Annie are not together anymore. Oh, by the way, she texted me earlier, wanted to know if you were okay."

"Annie texted you? Why hasn't she contacted me?"

"Probably because you've stupidly decided not to see her again before you leave?" Riley said rolling her eyes. "What about a glass of wine?"

Craig went through the ritual of opening a bottle of wine, but he kept mulling over his aunt's words. Annie with someone else. Annie kissing someone else. Annie making love with someone else…

"Um, Craig?" Riley chuckled, taking the bottle opener from him. "I've poured the wine. I'm just worried you might use this as a weapon."

"Let's eat," Aunt Janice said. "I've promised to make candy apples for the summer festival this weekend. I'll have to do it tonight, though. Tomorrow, after school, I'll be at the fairgrounds. Everyone lends a helping hand at these events."

"Anything I can do?" Craig asked.

"I'm sure they'd appreciate any help. And remember, Saturday night there's a dance. You two should get a date, go join the fun. Riley, you want to join us tomorrow?"

"I'll be at Annie's. I want to take more photos of the rooms and show Annie how her Instagram following is growing. She's been posting short videos of basic recipes and of her rooms and it seems to be a hit. Also, Vivian and I need to discuss what kind of pictures she wants on her wedding day. She's been so busy at the hospital, there hasn't been time."

Aunt Janice smiled. "That's next weekend, I can't believe their wedding day is finally here. I'm so happy for Aiden. When I asked him to visit just before Valentine's Day, I just knew he and Vivian—What I mean is…"

"Aunt Janice." Riley grinned. "It's time to confess, don't you think? You have played matchmaker, haven't you?"

His aunt smiled serenely. "Don't be silly, my dear. The magic between those two doesn't need any help."

"Just so you know, I'm watching you," Riley said sternly. "Be happy Aiden is getting married and don't try and set me up, okay?"

"Of course not, my dear."

Riley was still staring at their aunt. "What about Craig? Have you lured him here specifically for Annie?"

"Really, Riley, I don't know where you get all your ideas. Annie needed help with advertising. Craig is in marketing. It is an obvious solution to ask him to help her. Besides, you've heard Craig—he and Annie are not interested in any kind of relationship. I'm so glad Vivian asked you to be a bridesmaid as well."

Riley laughed. "Changing the subject will not always help. I'll be the bridesmaid with the camera."

"I haven't seen yours and Annie's dresses yet."

"We're having our final fitting tomorrow morning. It's a pity you…"

Craig tuned out his cousin's voice. Annie in white—it was such a sudden clear picture, he had to blink. Wow. She'd be a stunning bride. All those brown curls hanging down her back, her eyes glowing, her smile beautiful. Damn it to hell…

"Mommy, why is Uncle Craig saying a bad word?" Dylan's voice penetrated his thoughts.

Riley chuckled. "I'm not sure, sweetie. Maybe he's realized what an idiot he is."

"What's an idiot, Mommy?"

"You're looking at it." Riley laughed. Picking up the little boy, she winked at Craig. "Don't be scared of being happy, coz. It suits you."

"I can't agree more. Come on, let's eat," Aunt Janice said. "Hopefully, your uncle will realize his mistake before it is too late."

Chapter Seventeen

ANNIE HAD JUST posted her latest video on Instagram when her doorbell rang on Friday afternoon. It had been a busy day with her guests arriving since early in the day. She'd just finished giving her guests tea and wasn't expecting anyone. It could be one of the neighbors, or maybe Janice. Annie hadn't seen the older woman since Wednesday.

She was simply going through the motions each day. Even though the week had been crazy. Not only did she have to prepare for her guests, Vivian and Aiden's house was finally finished and they'd started moving in. She and Mitch had pitched in to help and she'd made sure everyone had something to eat by dinnertime each day. In between, they'd also followed up on the arrangements for the wedding.

But even though her mind had been occupied with so many things, she still missed Craig. Desperately. That wasn't something that was going to change any time soon, she'd have to live with that for the rest of her life.

She and Vivian had made several trips to Bozeman to pick up curtains and lamps and crockery her sister had ordered while Aiden had spent most days at the house accepting the delivery of furniture they'd bought. He was keeping his apartment in Portland for the times he needed to go back for work.

Annie's first guests for the weekend had arrived the day before. Having her house filled with people was exactly as she'd imagined it—the house was just about vibrating with laughter and late-night talks. Although she was in her element baking and cooking for everyone, she was doing it with a heavy, aching heart. Missing Craig was so much worse than she'd anticipated.

"I'll get it," Mitch called from inside the house.

Minutes later, he showed Craig's mother into Annie's kitchen, his eyebrows raised in a question mark.

"I'm on my way to school—see you later," her brother called and was gone.

Annie was so stunned it took her a few moments to recover. "Mrs. O'Sullivan, please come in," she finally got out. "Have a seat. We've just had tea and there's still some in the pot, or do you prefer coffee?" She was babbling but couldn't seem to stop.

"Nothing for me, please, thanks, Annie. And remember, I'm Claire." Pulling out a chair, the older woman sat down. "I was wondering if you have a few moments?"

"Of course." Annie pulled out a chair opposite her. Why would Craig's mom want to talk to her?

"You and Craig … you feel something for my son?"

Annie opened and closed her mouth a few times before

she was able to get a word out. "I do, but we're not together. We're just friends."

"Your choice?"

"Neither one of us is interested in a long-term relationship or marriage."

"It doesn't have anything to do with me, but would you mind telling me why?"

"I was dumped weeks before I was going to marry my ex, so for a while there, I didn't think I'd ever want to go down that road again. And Craig, well ... you should talk to him."

Claire's eyes were swimming in tears. "Because we left him behind? I had to make the choice to stay or go with my husband. I felt I was also needed. Craig was so independent, I never thought leaving him would have a negative impact on him. I was crying so hard after we'd dropped him off, I couldn't even wave goodbye."

"Talk to Craig, tell him exactly that. I think all of you need to share your feelings with one another. He's a great guy and any woman would be lucky to be his wife."

Claire stood up. "Thanks, Annie. You said for a while there you haven't thought about getting married again. Has it changed?"

Her heart breaking, Annie also got up. "I've met Craig. Let me walk you to the front door."

As Craig's mom stepped out on to the porch, Annie touched her arm. "You know what I was thinking when we had dinner the other night at Grey's Saloon?"

"Why are we here?" Claire asked wryly.

"No. You should talk to each other. Really talk. Ask Craig how it made him feel when you left him behind."

Claire swallowed. "I'm not sure I want to know the answer to that one."

"May I be blunt?" Annie asked. Someone had to tell Craig's mother how leaving him behind made him feel. She doubted Craig would ever manage to tell them.

Claire's eyes were filled with tears, but she nodded.

"You probably had your reasons, but leaving Craig with someone else while you joined Doctors without Borders to help others broke his heart and his spirit. Never mind that he was with family and that you were out in the world doing good. At ten, you need your parents. He's been wondering all this time why you left him. The ten-year-old little boy decided it was because of something he'd done…"

"Of course, it wasn't!" Claire called out, dabbing at her eyes.

"He was angry and felt guilty because he was angry. You were doing good; you were helping other people."

Sniffling, Claire took a tissue from her bag. "So, how do we fix this?"

"I don't know. I just know you have to try. My parents are gone. One ordinary day, they were in the wrong place at the wrong time and were killed. I'd give anything for one more chat with them."

Claire stepped forward and hugged her. "I like you, Annie. You've got spunk."

"I like you, too." Annie smiled, returning the hug. "I'm sorry if I was harsh. I just want the best for Craig. If anyone deserves it, it's him."

"Thank you, Annie. And thank you for being honest. I hope we see each other soon."

"Me, too."

THE RENTAL CAR his parents were using was sitting in front of his aunt's house when Craig arrived back from a meeting in town Saturday right before lunch. For a moment, he considered turning around. That was not going to help. Besides, they were probably on their way to Yellowstone National Park. He would see them again at the wedding but once he was back at work in Portland, he'd be so busy, he'd have more than enough excuses not to see them.

His parents and his aunt were having tea in Aunt Janice's small living room.

His aunt put the teapot down when she saw him. "Craig, I'm so glad you're back." She gave him a hug. "I was just telling your parents about all the clients you now have in Marietta. How did your meeting go?"

"Fine, thanks, Aunt Janice. I had another call on my way here. I've really enjoyed helping business owners around town. It's very different to being in charge of an account, keeping the client happy, getting the job done within as short a time as possible within a budget. Helping folks around here is a breeze in comparison. Is Riley around?" At least if she and Dylan were there, he wouldn't have to be alone with his parents.

Aunt Janice shook her head, her eyes filled with sympathy. "They've gone to the Graff Hotel. She wants to get the lay of the land for the photo shoot with the bridal couple tomorrow." Aunt Janice turned to his parents. "Riley is the photographer for Aiden and Vivian's wedding."

Aunt Janice's phone rang. "Will you please excuse me? I'm supposed to help at the fair and I'm already late."

"Of course," his mom said. "We're actually here to talk to Craig. We're off to Yellowstone tomorrow, but we'll be back for the wedding."

"Okay, great—I look forward to seeing you again." She hugged his mom, leaned against his dad for a moment. "Hopefully, I'll be able to spend more time with my brother now that you've retired."

"That's the idea." His father grinned.

"Enjoy your trip!" And with a wave and her phone against her ear, his aunt disappeared, leaving him alone with his parents.

Craig poured himself a cup of tea. Not that he wanted any, really, but at least it was something to do.

"What time are you leaving?" he asked, taking a seat.

"Early tomorrow morning," his mom said. "But that's

not why we're here."

"Oh?"

"There's no turning back the clock and changing our decision to leave you behind with your uncle and aunt when you were ten," his dad said, his eyes on his hands. "At the time, we were sure about what we were doing. Only now..." He looked up, his eyes suspiciously bright. "Only now we've come to realize our leaving you behind hurt you. You're angry with us and rightly so. You're a fine young man and I'm so sorry I don't know you ... we don't know you. We've missed all the important events along the years while we selfishly focused on our careers. If you can forgive us, we would like to be a part of your life."

Craig sat back, stared at his dad. For such a long time, he'd envisioned this moment when he'd have a chance to tell his parents exactly how he blamed them for leaving him behind, how angry he was. But looking at both of them now, all he was feeling was regret for not having them around while he was growing up. The anger he'd carried with him for so long had vanished over the last few days.

"We've hurt you," his mom said softly. "We've never really talked about how you felt at the time. Can you tell us?"

Craig looked at his mother. She really wanted to know. He wouldn't have been able to express his feelings in words if it hadn't been for Annie. She'd helped him to put his hurt and anger into words. "I thought I'd done something wrong. That you didn't want me."

"Is that why you don't think you should get married?"

"I don't get how you could leave me behind without a backward glance. I don't want to ever have to leave a kid of mine behind. I was angry and felt guilty because I was angry. You were out in the world, saving lives."

His mom's eyes were wet with tears. "You haven't done anything wrong. We love you. We're so proud of you. And I'm so sorry we've made you feel unwanted and guilty. Do you think you could ever forgive us? And just for the record? You're clearly your own man. You stepped in when your uncle Sean died. You were helping out, supporting Aiden and Riley when Cara became ill, and after her death, you continued to help your cousins. Riley has told me how you'd moved in with her to help look after Dylan. You'd be a great husband and dad, Craig. You've been that for Aiden and Riley over the last few years."

Staring at his mother, her words reverberated in his heart. She was so right, he was his own man. He'd never do what they'd done and leave anyone he loved behind. He'd protect those he loved with his last breath.

A weight had been lifted off of his chest somehow.

His thoughts racing, he nodded. "I'd like to forgive you and, yes, it would be nice to have you in my life, but we'd have to get to know each other and I have to learn to trust you again. I've been angry for a long time, though, so it'll probably take time."

Sniffling, his mom reached over to touch him. "We understand that. We're willing to do the work, Craig. You're important to us."

"And just so you know," his dad said, "every time we left you behind, your mom cried so much, she couldn't turn around and wave. I know it's no consolation, but ..."

Swallowing against the lump in his throat, Craig cleared his throat. "I don't know if I'll ever understand why you did what you did, and I'll have more questions along the way, but can we now please talk about something else besides feelings?"

"Thank goodness," his dad said, rubbing his eyes. "I'm getting a headache."

"Tell me about your trip?" he asked.

His dad was clearly relieved to have something else to talk about and pulled out his phone to show him a map. His mom chipped in and when they stood up to leave half an hour later, everyone was smiling.

Craig walked them out to their car.

His mom gave him a hug. "We're going to book rooms at Annie's for the wedding. She's such a lovely person."

"She is."

"I saw her yesterday," his mom said as she got into the car.

"I was wondering how you know I don't want to get married."

His mother grimaced. "Your Annie is very passionate. She didn't pull any punches and told me exactly what our leaving you behind did to you. Because of her, we're here today, trying to right our wrongs. Another thing—she told me she'd thought for a while she doesn't want to get married either."

Frowning, he softly repeated his mom's words. "For a while? Is that what she said?"

"That's what she said. But apparently, she then met someone. Although she hadn't said it in so many words, it sounded as if she's now changed her mind."

His dad started the car and, with a final wave, they drove off. Frowning, his heart beating like crazy, Craig stood staring after them.

The churning inside of him was back, as if something was trying to fall into place.

BY SIX O'CLOCK on Saturday night, Annie was finally able to catch her breath. All her guests were going to the dance at the fairgrounds tonight. She'd made a quiche for those who wanted to eat something before they went and had just cleaned the kitchen and prepared everything for tomorrow morning's breakfast.

As she ran up the stairs to her room, she was smiling. She really loved having people here. The small B and B was alive with chatter and laughter, just the way she'd imagined. Her Instagram account was growing daily—all because of Craig.

There wasn't a minute in a day she didn't feel like calling him and telling him how much he'd helped her.

And there he was in her thoughts again. She'd been so busy since Wednesday but the problem with cooking and baking and preparing rooms meant her thoughts were free to roam wherever they wanted to. Where they roamed to was Craig. Always Craig. And how much she loved him.

Sleep had been impossible since she'd seen him last. Every time she closed her eyes, she swore she could feel Craig breathing next to her. His scent still lingered in her office even though she'd left the windows wide open for most of Thursday.

She hadn't planned on going to the dance, but Hunter was going to pick her up. She'd bumped into him when she went shopping yesterday and, minutes later, she'd found herself agreeing to go to the dance with him. She'd been upfront with him and told him she could only go as a friend and he'd agreed. He really was such a nice guy.

Going out tonight, when her whole being wanted to be with Craig, was really the last thing she wanted to do. Sitting at home, crying her eyes out, also held very little appeal.

Inhaling deeply, she marched toward her closet. She had a new red dress and a pair of red killer heels she'd bought in Bozeman yesterday when she'd accompanied Vivian, who still needed things for her honeymoon. So, she was going to enjoy her evening, come hell or high water.

Clenching her teeth, she went to the bathroom and

opened the shower tap. As the water streamed over her face, the tears started. Leaning against the tiles, she dropped her head and sobbed. This was exactly why she'd taken that vow after Ted had dropped her not to open her heart to anyone again.

But then Craig hugged her, putting all her broken pieces together. But now her heart had shattered into so many tiny fragments she was afraid there was no healing to be done.

Almost like Humpty Dumpty.

Giggling through her tears at her own silliness, she lifted her head up to the cascading water.

She'd been happy before Craig, damn it, she could learn to be again.

"I THOUGHT AT least one of you would have a date for the dance," Aunt Janice said as Craig parked his car at the fairgrounds.

"You're our date," Riley chuckled as they got out of the car.

"Well, at least Annie has a date, I hear," his aunt said. "Apparently, Carol Bingley overheard Hunter telling someone in the pharmacy he was taking Annie to the dance."

Craig gnashed his teeth.

"Oh?" Riley smiled as they began walking toward a big barn from where music could be heard.

"He's a sweet man and he'll be good to her."

With his blood roaring in his ears, Craig followed his aunt and cousin. Dylan was on his arm and chatting away, but Craig wasn't listening. Annie with another man—the mere thought had him seeing red.

He saw Annie the moment they entered the barn. She was laughing up at the big cowboy twirling her around and around, her brown curls bobbing up and down to the rhythm of her body. The red dress she was wearing ended way above her knee, showing off those long, silky legs. The same legs he'd touched, the same legs that had been wrapped around him. And damn, those heels.

As he stared at her, he recognized the song.

And in whose arms you're gonna be
So, darlin', save the last dance for me, hmm

She should be dancing with him; she should be in his arms. That was where Annie belonged.

Somewhere between openly talking about her reaction to him, her problems with her B and B, her gorgeous smile, she'd eased the ache around his heart and helped him deal with his own baggage. She'd listened, she'd laughed with him, she'd made love with him.

The churning inside him grinded to a staggering halt and the pieces of a messy puzzle finally fell into place. He nearly groaned aloud. He'd been so damn stupid.

You're breaking my heart. Those had been Annie's words.

That meant she loved him. She wouldn't have slept with him if she didn't love him. And he was in love with her. Crazily in love with her.

It was all so crystal clear in that moment. Why the hell had it taken him so long to understand what his heart had been telling him all along? Now, when she was in someone else's arms? He wanted to be with her. He needed to be with her. She made him a better man. Through her eyes he was a better man.

Without taking his eyes off the couple, he handed Dylan to Riley.

"Craig…" his aunt said.

"Not a good idea, coz," Riley said, grabbing hold of his arm. "You don't want to make another scene. And please spare Annie more gossip. Look around you. People are watching."

Inhaling deeply, Craig became aware of where he was and, yes, people were watching. Damn small towns.

"I love her."

His aunt touched his arm. "Of course, you do, my dear." She sighed. "Seriously, men. I don't know why it always takes you so long to figure out what the heart wants. I can't tell you how it warms my heart. Annie makes you happy and you so deserve to be happy. But Riley is right. This is not the place or time to make another scene. Go home, cool off, talk to her in the morning."

ANNIE KNEW THE exact moment Craig stepped into the barn. She wasn't facing the door, but the slight shiver down her spine she always felt when he was near was enough to alert her to his presence.

As Hunter swung her around, she met Craig's eyes across the room. Hands on hips, a deep frown on his forehead, he was watching her. For a moment longer he stood like that before he turned around and walked right back out.

Her heart breaking, she closed her eyes as Hunter swung her out for a last turn. The song was ending. What was she doing here, dancing with someone else when her whole being wanted to be with Craig?

"Hunter..."

Smiling wryly, he chuckled. "You want to leave."

"I'm sorry."

Shrugging, he steered her toward their table. "Your heart belongs to someone else. Get your bag, I'll take you back."

"That's not necessary..."

"My momma would skin me alive if I let a lady walk home this time of night."

Annie swallowed back her tears. Here she was with a nice, attractive guy who made it clear he wanted to be with her, but her heart wasn't here. It had left with Craig.

He was who her whole being wanted, nobody else.

Chapter Eighteen

CRAIG UNLOCKED THE front door to Aunt Janice's house, but instead of entering, he closed it again. He needed space to figure out a few things. Riley had just dropped him off, she was going back to the dance where their aunt and Dylan still were.

With his hands deep in his jacket pockets, he walked down the street, his eyes on his feet. Of course, he damn well loved Annie. He'd probably fallen for her gorgeous smile back in February when he and Riley were here.

She was everything he never knew he wanted. She was kind, open, funny, gorgeous and so sexy he couldn't see straight. There was no way he could go back to Portland before he told her how he felt.

And then what? He slowed down, stopped. Riley was right, there was nothing to say they had to get married, but what about Annie? How would she feel about it? Annie in white … the picture had been so clear, what if …

"Fancy meeting you here," a soft voice said close by.

He looked up. His heart just about leapt out of his body. Annie. She was on the sidewalk in front of her house.

Although she was wearing a coat, those sexy heels were still on her feet. Somewhere behind them a car drove away.

"You're in front of my house," Annie said. "Again."

His hands still deep in his pockets, he walked right up to her. "I always seem to end up here, on the street where you live."

Her eyes were hooded, her face for once giving nothing away. "Why do you think that is?"

"It took me a while, but I've finally figured it out to-night."

"Yeah?"

"Yeah."

His gaze slid over every inch of her lovely face. "I've missed you."

The corners of her mouth turned upward, ever so slight-ly. Her eyes softened. "I've missed you, too."

"I don't ever want to be without you again."

"Yeah?"

"Yeah?"

"Details?"

"Don't have them yet."

"Okay. Wanna come in?"

"If I do, I won't be leaving. Ever."

"Why?" Those gorgeous brown eyes weren't giving him an out.

Slowly, he took his hands out of his pockets and cupped her face. "Because, beautiful Annie, you and me? It's a forever kind of thing. It's always been you, long before I've even met you."

"Why?" she persisted.

And, finally, he knew what she wanted to hear. "Because I love that you love cooking and making people happy. Because I love your smile, because I love how you say everything you're thinking, because I love that you get me, but mostly, Annie, because I love you."

A beautiful smile lit up her face. "Oh, that is so corny, but I love it."

Laughing out loud, he picked her up. "And I love how you make me laugh." With long strides, he walked toward the front door.

Annie's arms circled his neck. "I love you, too."

"I know."

Gasping, she lifted her head. "How could you know?"

"You wouldn't have made love with me if you hadn't loved me. And you told me I was breaking your heart. Stupidly, it took me a few days to figure out what that meant."

Sighing, she rested her head against his shoulder again. "You know me so well."

"Is the door locked or…"

The front door flew open. Mitch stood there, hands on hips, his eyes slits, his nostrils flaring. Seriously. The brother. But, okay, this was as good a time to deal with him and tell him what was going you. "Mitch, good to see you. I'd like to stay and chat, but as you can see, I've got my hands full." He tried to move past Mitch, but he should've known he wasn't going to get off so easily.

"Not so quick, O'Sullivan. What are you doing with my sister?"

Grinning, Craig looked down at Annie. "I don't think you want to know. But…" he added just before Mitch exploded, "I love her and I never want to be without her again."

Mitch exhaled slowly. "Well, hell. I don't know if I like it."

"Too bad. I'm not going anywhere."

After several tense seconds, Mitch looked at Annie. "This what you want?"

"I love him. So, yes, this is exactly what I want."

Mitch's eyes were on Craig again. "But I'll be watching you. You make her cry, just once and…"

"I'll probably screw up once in a while, but it won't be because I don't love her."

Mitch began to turn away, but Annie grabbed his arm. "And just so you know, you don't have to go anywhere. This is your house as well."

Mitch shook his head. "Thanks, sis, but I've been looking around and I think I've found a place." He pinned Craig down with a stare. "Quite close by, so I can keep an eye on you O'Sullivans." And still muttering, Mitch turned and stomped away.

"Your room?" he asked. "I love holding you like this, but I am thirty-six, you know."

"I'll keep you young, don't worry." Annie laughed. "Up the stairs to the right. And it's our room now."

Taking the stairs two at a time, he held his precious cargo close to his body. "We have a lot to talk about. I'll get an office in town, we can…"

"This one," she said, pointing to the first room. "We can talk but not tonight." Annie smiled as he let her slide to the floor. "First…" she said, dropping her coat to the floor. "We have to deal with the beading and throbbing, don't you—"

He didn't give her time to finish her sentence. Swooping down, he captured her lips in a searing kiss. Now that he knew why he couldn't get enough of her, he couldn't wait to show her exactly how much he loved her.

"This dress has to come off," he murmured against her lips.

She turned around. "Zipper…"

As CRAIG SLID down the zipper of her dress slowly, he bent down to taste her. Following the downward movement of the zipper, his mouth trailed behind, leaving hot kisses all over her skin.

By the time her dressed pooled at her feet, she was shivering. From anticipation, from excitement, from need for the man standing behind her.

"No bra," he whispered, cupping her breasts.

"The dress…" she began, but his hands trailed down her body and she forgot what she'd wanted to say. Her head dropped back against his rock-hard body as she gave herself up to his hands.

Only when she was shuddering did he stop and gently lead her to the bed.

"Keep your shoes on." He grinned as he gently picked her up and laid her down on the bed. "It nearly killed me watching you dance in these with another man."

"That was before I knew you loved me."

His eyes nearly black with desire, he kissed her slowly. "Now you know."

"Now I know," she whispered.

His breath not quite steady, he quickly got rid of his clothes. Leaning back on her elbows she watched him. By the time he joined her on the bed, she was on fire for him.

Pushing him down, she straddled him. "My turn to love you. And I'm sorry, I have to get rid of the shoes, they're going to do someone some serious bodily harm."

"I hope you'll wear them often."

"Promise."

IN AWE, HE watched as Annie's head bent down over him.

Her warm lips traveled over his body, caressing every inch, tormenting him, moving lower and lower, sending his blood to boiling point within seconds. Those clever hands were also busy. Touching, fondling, loving him. His pulse was racing like a drumbeat.

"Mmm, there's a lot of throbbing going on here, I see." Annie chuckled as her hand closed around him.

For a moment, he reveled in her touch, but he wasn't going to last if she continued doing that. Flipping her over, he leaned over her. "I don't want this to be over too soon..."

"Well, baby..." She grinned as one of her hands went right back to where it had been. "This is where I have to tell you if you're going to stay with me, you're not always going to get your way."

His only defense was to haul her closer and kiss her again. As his tongue shot through to the depths of her mouth to find hers, heat slammed into him, his breath strangling in his throat. Frantically, possessively, his hand moved down her body, worshipping her slick flesh. He'd never get enough of her.

Smooth lines, silky limbs, soft curves. Hot, irresistible. Breathing in her flowery scent, he tried to rein in his galloping libido. This was for her. Showing her how intensely he craved her, how deeply he loved her, couldn't be done in the span of a few minutes.

Only when her body arched restlessly up into his, her breathing ragged, did he cup her heat. Her moan was low, broken, echoing through his body. Lifting his head, he watched her eyes glaze over as she reached the first pinnacle. Fascinated, he stared at her as she soared. Beautiful, she was so, so beautiful.

When minutes later, her eyes finally fluttered opened, he hoisted himself above her, his muscles quivering as he slid over her. He'd never wanted anyone as he wanted this woman. Need for her pulsed through his body, clawed at his throat.

With his eyes on hers, he linked their fingers as he slipped inside her. Her heat welcomed him, fitted around him like a glove. He was home. Finally.

ANNIE TRIED TO keep her eyes on Craig, but desire built again quickly, blurring her vision. Sensation after delicious sensation broke over her. The sound of neighbors going about their nightly routines was far away. Within the cocoon she and Craig had created, she barely registered anything else. Seeped in his scent, all she could hear was their labored breathing, all she could feel was his body moving inside her, taking her higher and higher up a steep mountain.

Fighting back the mists, she opened her eyes. All their walls were down, the hurt healed. She wanted to savor this moment they became one. His head was thrown back as he rode with her, faster and faster until a red haze again blurred her vision and she surrendered.

Hearing Craig shouting out her name, finally sent her over the cliff as she pulled him close to her. She'd never been so vulnerable, never felt so beautiful, never been so strong.

"WHY ARE YOU sneaking out of the house?"

Craig's hand was on the front doorknob. Cussing softly, he turned around to face Vivian. He'd hoped everyone was still asleep.

Vivian was coming down the stairs, hand on hip, glaring at him. "I'm waiting for your answer. And it better be a damn good one. You've been with Annie."

"Exactly. I love her. Which is why—"

Inhaling sharply, Vivian walked right up to him. "If you're telling me you have to go because you love her, I'm going to clobber you."

"Which is why I have to go to Bozeman."

"Why?"

"It's a surprise."

"For Annie?"

"Yes."

"You really love her?"

He couldn't help the smile if he'd tried. "I do."

"And that's why you have to go to Bozeman?"

"Yes."

She exhaled slowly. "Do you need my help?"

"I've got this. I know Annie."

Finally grinning, she threw her arms around his neck. "I'm so happy for you two."

"Why are my soon-to-be wife's arms around my cousin?" Aiden asked as he came jogging down the steps.

Vivian clapped her hands. "He loves Annie."

Chuckling, Aiden slapped him on the shoulder. "I could've told you that days ago. So where are you off to?"

"Bozeman."

Aiden stared at him. "To Bozeman to..." And then he smiled. "Of course. Glad you saw the light. Care for some company?"

"Yeah, that would be great."

"You've told Annie where you're off to?" Vivian asked.

"Well, no. She's still sleeping. Besides, I don't want to spoil the surprise."

"She's going to wake up and you won't be there."

Craig frowned. "Surely, she'll know I'll be back?"

Rolling her eyes, Vivian groaned. "Seriously. You're worse than Aiden. You were with her last night; this morning you're gone. You want her to jump to the wrong conclusions or ...?"

"I'll tell her I'll be back." He grinned, quickly texting her.

"Good thinking," Vivian said drily.

Chuckling, Aiden patted him on the shoulder. "You still

have a lot to learn."

His cousin was right, he probably had a lot still to learn. What he had discovered over the last few days, however, was that he could be a husband, a father. Most of all, he wanted to be Annie's husband and, if it were to happen, a father to their children. With Annie by his side, he could do anything.

HER EYES STILL closed, Annie turned on her side, her hand reaching for Craig. But he wasn't there. Not quite awake yet, she sat up, pulling the sheet over herself. It was a bit disconcerting waking up alone, stark naked. Blinking, she looked around her room.

Her red dress was neatly folded over the chair, the red shoes placed on the floor next to it, but there was no sign of Craig's clothes. If not for the faint traces of his scent, she'd be worried she might have dreamt last night.

Her phone bleeped and she quickly grabbed it. It was a message from Craig.

I love you. Errand to run.

Sighing, she got up, pulled on a sweater and jeans and opened the windows. Inhaling the fresh air, she hugged herself. She was happy. Really happy. What a giddy feeling.

"Annie?" Vivian called out softly as she opened the door, tray in hand.

Annie sniffed in the air. "Is that coffee? Thank you, but you're the soon-to-be bride. I need to be pampering you, not the other way around."

Grinning, Vivian put the tray on a small table before she sat on the bed next to Annie. "Get into bed, I want to spoil you for a change. You're always spoiling me. I've also made scones. Not yours, I'm afraid, but from what I've heard, you need some nourishment this morning."

Annie climbed on to her bed. "You've seen Craig?"

"Indeed, I have."

"Where is he?"

"Hasn't he texted you?"

"He did, but I don't understand where he's off to at this hour. Last night…" Sighing, Annie hugged herself. "He loves me, Viv."

Vivian leaned forward, hugging her. "Of course, he does. It's been so obvious the two of you are crazy about each other." She handed her a mug and a plate of scones. "Eat, drink, and tell me all about it. Who said what? Who said it first? Come on, I want to know everything."

Chapter Nineteen

VIVIAN'S WEDDING DAY had broken with the smell of spring in the air and from there on it had been a glorious day. Craig's parents had arrived the day before and his mom had accompanied all of them to the Graff on Friday afternoon to check whether everything was ready for the big day.

Annie took a breath and stared at herself in the mirror. Her big sister was getting married. She was so happy for her.

The bride was dressed and was looking absolutely gorgeous. Riley was with her at the moment, making sure Vivian had everything she needed and taking more pictures. It had been a chaotic morning getting everyone ready. Riley had called on Marlene and Sienna Murphy to help with the makeup and hair, and they'd spent the morning together taking turns to laugh and cry.

Annie closed her eyes, blinking away a few tears. The lingering sadness, she knew, would pass. Both she and Vivian would've given anything to have their parents here today, but they'd found a new family in Marietta with Janice and her godchildren. They had a lot to be grateful for.

Inhaling, Annie pressed her hand to her tummy where the butterflies hadn't stopped moving since last Saturday night. She still didn't know why Craig had left her alone in bed on Sunday morning; he kept telling her she had to wait, it was a surprise.

Because of the crazy week, she and Craig rarely had time to talk, let alone discuss their future together. Although, he'd said he never wanted to be without her, she knew not to take it literally. His life and work were in Portland. They'd probably need to talk about how everything would work, but she couldn't really be bothered.

She and Craig were together. Marriage had never been on the table, she'd made her peace with that. The fact that she'd changed her mind and would marry Craig in a heartbeat didn't mean he'd also suddenly feel the same way. She understood why and she'd accepted it. As long as she could see him from time to time, she'd be happy.

She had her B and B. She even had a growing following on Instagram. It had been a process, but she now enjoyed sharing recipes and glimpses of her house with strangers online.

There was a knock on her door. "Annie?" Aiden called.

It was Aiden and he sounded frantic. Annie hurried to the door and opened it.

"They don't want me to see Vivian!" Aiden just about wailed. "I want to give her this, but for some or other insane reason, I can't see her."

Annie took the small box from him. "I'll make sure she gets it. You have to get to the church, we'll see you in"—she looked at her watch—"twenty minutes."

Craig appeared at the top of the stairs. "Aiden, where the…" he began, but then his eyes fell on Annie. Grinning, he rushed toward her. "Look at you …" Pulling her closer, his eyes skimmed over her before he kissed her.

"Come on, lover boy." Aiden chuckled. "We both will have to cool our heels. Get my bride to me as soon as possible, please?"

With a last quick kiss and a devastating smile, Craig left with Aiden. Leaning against the wall, Annie put a hand to her tummy where the butterflies were going crazy.

Goodness, those steamy romances she'd been reading didn't come close to the real thing.

The door to Vivian's bedroom flew open. Riley came out. "That the present from Aiden?"

"Yes, he's very frustrated." Annie grinned.

"So am I," Vivian cried. "What a ridiculous idea. I want to see him. I want to make sure he hasn't changed his mind. Maybe he's changed his mind. I won't blame him. I mean this is crazy and—"

Riley grabbed her hands. "He hasn't changed his mind. My brother is hopelessly in love with you. Come on, breathe. Just breathe."

Annie handed Vivian the small package Aiden had left. "I have a present for you. From your bridegroom."

Vivian stared at the box. "He can't give me more things. He's done so much already."

Riley led Vivian back into the room. "Of course, he can. Come on, sit down. You haven't even seen what it is." She pushed Vivian down in front of her mirror. "Open it up."

Vivian opened the small box and inhaled deeply. Her eyes filled with tears. "It's beautiful," she got out as a lone tear ran down her face.

"No crying, for heaven's sake," Riley scolded, although her own eyes were quite bright with tears. "Annie, tissue, please. Marlene and Sienna have left already. Sapphire and diamond earrings to match your wedding band—how beautiful and thoughtful. Didn't know my brother had it in him. You bring out the best in him, Vivian, I'm so glad he met you."

"So am I," sniffled Vivian, blinking furiously.

Annie handed Vivian a tissue. "Just dab below your eyes and inhale deeply. If you cry, I'll cry and we'll ruin everything Marlene and Sienna worked so hard to create. And you look so beautiful."

"The satin dress in classic lines is so you," Riley agreed. "Come on, people, we have a wedding to go to!"

But by the time they finally got into the car, all three of them were still blinking away tears.

CRAIG HAD BIDED his time, but he wasn't waiting any longer. With a nod to the band, he made his way to where Annie was chatting to his parents and aunt. The speeches had been made, the cake cut. Everybody had had dinner.

The happy couple had given him his blessing to make his move. Initially, he'd thought to do it only after the wedding, but Vivian had insisted he do it at the end of the evening when everyone was still there.

The first notes of the song filled the hall of the Graff Hotel. The lead singer, a cowboy on one of the ranches around Marietta bent his head and crooned into the microphone.

You can dance every dance with the guy

He held out his hand to Annie. "Will you dance with me, Annie?"

Her brilliant smile lit up her face as she moved toward him. He swung her out before pulling her close to his heart.

So, darlin', save the last dance for me

"Will you do that?" he asked, looking down into her brown eyes.

"Do what?"

"Save every last dance for me?"

"Of course."

"Remember I said we have to talk?"

Her smile slipped a notch. "When are you leaving?"

"I told you I never want to be without you again."

"With you working in Portland, it's not practical, silly." She smiled. "We'll figure it out as we go along."

"I've already figured it out. I'm never leaving my wife."

Her steps faltered, she stilled. "Wife?"

With his eyes on her, he took out the small box that had been burning his pocket for the last six days and dropped down on his one knee. The band stopped playing, everyone stopped talking and moved around them in a circle.

Annie's eyes widened. "Craig?"

"Annie Miller, I want to be with you, marry you, make babies with you, and I always, always want you to save the very last dance for me. Will you please marry me?"

One after the other, emotions flitted over her face—surprise, worry, wonder.

With a laugh, she pulled him up, her eyes never leaving his face. "I'd love to marry you, Craig," she said, holding out her hand.

Under whistles and laughter and clapping, he slipped the ring he'd bought in Bozeman last Sunday on her finger.

Her eyes wet with tears, she held up her hand. "Diamonds forming a small heart—you know me so well. I love it."

"I was thinking about all those romances you love to read." He grinned.

"You're sure about this?" she asked, her arms circling his neck. "There's going to be lots of beading and throbbing," she whispered in his ear.

Pulling her closer, he burst out laughing. "I'm counting on it."

IT WAS LATE before they all gathered in Annie's kitchen for a final toast. The bride and groom were leaving the next day early to catch their flight in Bozeman to their honeymoon destination.

Smiling, Annie hugged her sister. "I'm so sorry we stole your show, but I'm so happy!"

Laughing, Vivian put down her champagne glass and grabbed Annie's hand. "Craig wanted to wait till after the wedding, but I didn't want to miss it. Show me your ring again." She smiled and picked up Annie's hand. "It's so you, Annie, I love it. I offered to help, but he assured me he knew what you'd like."

Over Vivian's head, Annie met Craig's eyes. "Yeah, he does. I'm a lucky girl."

"I'm the lucky one," Craig insisted as he walked over and pulled her close. "So, if you'll excuse us…"

"Wait a minute." Aunt Janice stopped them. "We haven't talked about the when and where of your wedding."

"The where is easy," Craig said. "We do what Vivian and Aiden have done, have it in the Graff Hotel. They throw a nice party. Baby? Do you want something else?" He looked down at Annie.

Annie nodded. "I'm happy with that."

"When?" asked Riley. "What about a Christmas wedding?"

Craig was shaking his head even before she'd finished talking. "There's no way I'm waiting that long."

"What about the beginning of August?" Annie asked. "It'll give us enough time to prepare. I love fall. The weather is perfect that time of year."

"That's still two months away but if that's what you want, okay," Craig said. "But make it the first weekend, okay?"

"Okay." She laughed.

Craig's mother touched Annie's hand. "Please let me know if there is anything I can do."

Annie gave her a hug. "Clear your calendar two weeks before the time and come and stay with us?"

"We'd like that," Craig's dad said.

Craig took her hand. "Okay, anything else?"

Vivian laughed. "There is a lot to talk about, but go. We'll figure out the rest when Aiden and I return from our honeymoon."

"Good night, everyone," Aiden said, taking Vivian's hand. "I'm taking my bride to our house."

"And I'm taking my fiancé to our room," Craig chuckled.

ANNIE CLOSED THE bathroom door behind her and stepped into her room. Her eyes fell on the bed. She laughed. Craig was nowhere to be seen, but the bed had been stripped and was now covered in midnight-black sheets—exactly like the ones in her steamy dreams.

Hugging herself, she smiled. She was tired, it had been a crazy week and an even crazier day, but the joy inside of her was giving her renewed energy. Walking toward the window, she looked up at Copper Mountain, its dark, steady presence barely visible.

The move to Marietta had been a leap into the unknown for her and Mitch and Vivian. They hadn't known anybody; they'd left everything they'd owned behind. After Ted, she'd just wanted to get as far away as possible from Sacramento and falling for someone else simply hadn't been in any of her many plans.

But then Craig hugged her and even though she hadn't known it at the time, that hug had been the first step in healing all her pain.

The bedroom door opened behind her and there he was. Her heart melted. In his hands was the biggest bunch of red roses she'd ever seen. Her favorite flower.

"Are those for me?" She sighed, holding out her hands. "They're gorgeous, but where on earth did you get so many red roses this time of year? It must've be so expensive!"

Putting the roses in her arms, he cupped her face. "I've

spent years just working, so now I can spoil you whenever I want. Risa Davidson, who owns the floral shop in town, is a miracle worker. She made it possible for me to get you your favorite flower."

"How do you know her?"

"She stood behind me in the pharmacy the day I bought the condoms."

Annie burst out laughing. "That's one way to meet people." She put the roses on a chair nearby before she stepped into his arms. "Thank you for my ring and the roses, but I don't need the grand gestures. All I need is you on those midnight-black sheets you've put on the bed."

"You like?" He grinned.

"My steamy dreams come true."

"We have so much to talk about..."

She pulled her pajama top over her head. "Not now. Talking will have to wait for tomorrow. I've saved you the last dance, baby."

With a laugh, he picked her up and took her to the bed. As he bent down to kiss her, she sighed. "No storybook hero could ever be as dashing, caring, and sexy as the one I'm engaged to," she whispered against his lips.

"Well, I'll have to check. I need proof," he said, cupping her breast. "Obviously, I'm doing something right. There is some serious beading going on here, Miss Annie."

Grinning, her hand closed around him. "And I'm very

happy to report there is major throbbing as well. I think we have a bestseller."

With a laugh, he gathered her close. "I love our dance."

And then he kissed her.

The End

Want more? Don't miss Mitch and Riley's story in
Merry Christmas, Montana!

Join Tule Publishing's newsletter for more great reads and weekly deals!

Acknowledgements

A big thank you to the lovely ladies at Tule Publishing for all their support and help, especially to Kelly Hunter who has helped me find a place for my characters in Marietta, Montana. It has been such a pleasure working with her.

I've fallen in love with Marietta, the endearing and even the not-so-endearing characters, thank you for letting me add another family to this make-believe town.

A big thank you to Kathleen Bosman, a very helpful Beta reader for reading through the first draft.

And to all the readers and bloggers out there – thank you so much for all your lovely feedback and messages – it's so nice to hear from you.

And as always, thanks to Theo, my husband, for his continued and enthusiastic support and help.

If you enjoyed *A Match Made in Montana*,
you'll love the next book in…

The Millers of Marietta series

Book 1: *My Montana Valentine*

Book 2: *A Match Made in Montana*

Book 3: *Merry Christmas, Montana*
Coming in October 2023

More Books by Elsa Winckler

The Cavallo Brothers series

Book 1: *An Impossible Attraction*

Book 2: *An Irresistible Temptation*

Book 3: *The Ultimate Surrender*

About the Author

I have been reading love stories for as long as I can remember and when I 'met' the classic authors like Jane Austen, Elizabeth Gaskell, Henry James The Brontë sisters, etc. during my Honours studies, I was hooked for life.

I married my college boyfriend and soul mate and after 43 years, 3 interesting and wonderful children and 3 beautiful grandchildren, he still makes me weak in the knees. We are fortunate to live in the picturesque little seaside village of Betty's Bay, South Africa with the ocean a block away and a beautiful mountain right behind us. And although life so far has not always been an easy ride, it has always been an exciting and interesting one!

I like the heroines in my stories to be beautiful, feisty, independent and headstrong. And the heroes must be strong but possess a generous amount of sensitivity. They are of course, also gorgeous! My stories typically incorporate the family background of the characters to better understand where they come from and who they are when we meet them in the story.

Thank you for reading

A Match Made in Montana

If you enjoyed this book, you can find more from all our great authors at TulePublishing.com, or from your favorite online retailer.

TULE
PUBLISHING